A ONE-ARMED BANDIT . . .

"Freeze!"

Ruff froze. His eyes whipped from the one-armed man to the farmhouse, which the five riders had stormed. There were two more shots. Ruff felt his heart hammer violently against his chest. His hands clenched into fists. He glanced at Houston, and his brother was as white as the snow at their feet.

"You boys got any money or anything of value on your persons?"

"Got some money," Houston said, "but not much."

Two more shots banked across the snow-covered pasture . . .

"You got anything of value?" the leader said, jerking his carbine in Ruff's direction.

Ruff's mind spun like a coin. His first impulse was to say no, but something told him that would be a fatal mistake.

"I got a little money and a watch and chain. It belonged to my father."

"Now it's gonna belong to me," the one-armed man said with a cruel smile. "Let's see it."

Ruff reached for the top button of his coat and as he did, his hand whipped up, snatched his hat from his head, and he swatted the one-armed man's horse across the eyes.

The animal whirled away in fright and Ruff threw himself at the one-armed man . . .

SPECIAL PREVIEW!

Turn to _____ xcerpt from an _____

. . . The _____ ud by America _____ Giles Tippette.

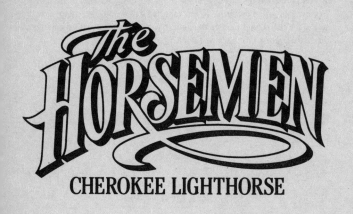

THE HORSEMEN

CHEROKEE LIGHTHORSE

GARY McCARTHY

DIAMOND BOOKS, NEW YORK

CHEROKEE LIGHTHORSE

A Diamond Book / published by arrangement with
the author

PRINTING HISTORY
Diamond edition / October 1992

ISBN: 1-55773-797-5

Diamond Books are published by The Berkley Publishing
Group, 200 Madison Avenue, New York, New York 10016.
The name "DIAMOND" and its logo are trademarks
belonging to Charter Communications, Inc.

PRINTED IN THE UNITED STATES OF AMERICA

10 9 8 7 6 5 4 3 2 1

ONE

Rufus "Ruff" Ballou reined his exhausted Thoroughbred stallion to a halt and anxiously waited for his brother and sister. He would be eighteen in a month, but trail weariness and deep lines of fatigue made him appear ten years older. Ruff was very tall and slender, all sharp corners and angles just like his young Thoroughbred stallion. High Fire stood better than sixteen hands and Ruff's legs gripped the barrel of his magnificent stallion with the grace and naturalness of a man born to the saddle. Ruff's mane of thick black hair exploded out from under the wide brim of his felt hat and his big right hand gripped an Enfield rifle while his left held a pair of soft latigo reins with the same unconscious ease a bookkeeper might hold a pencil.

Ruff's hooded and restless eyes snapped from tree to tree, measuring shadows, seeking movement and danger. Arkansas was a contested land, a blood-soaked and violent Civil War battleground where a few Reb patrols still eluded the plundering Union armies.

As Ruff waited, High Fire shifted nervously on a thick ground cover of decaying leaves, its hooves raking black, pungent slashes through centuries old humus. In the naked branches of a sycamore tree seventy feet overhead, a crow strutted and raucously berated the invaders on horses.

Ruff pushed back the brim of his sweat-stained hat and watched the arrogant bird. He could have drawn the Colt on his hip and blasted the crow to eternity, but instead he appreciated the crow for telling him that he and his family were the only forest intruders close at hand.

1

After several moments, Ruff glanced back at his brother and sister, who were leading the last four Ballou mares out of Tennessee. One of the mares was round-bellied with foal and she was slowing them all down. That was all right. Perhaps the mare would produce an outstanding Thoroughbred runner able to win them a fortune in the West.

As he watched for danger, Ruff's hand slipped down to High Fire's smoothly muscled shoulder and he spoke to the chestnut stallion in a nonsensical but pleasant sounding blend of Cherokee and English. Ruff's late father, Justin Ballou, had been a horse talker, too, a man who had communicated with horses using unrelated words. It had been Justin who'd shown by example how subtle inflection, lilt, timbre, and resonance could calm a horse while an angry but not necessarily loud tone had just the opposite effect. Justin believed a man could read a horse's thoughts mostly by the position and movement of its ears.

Now High Fire was listening, ears pricked attentively to every nuance of Ruff's familiar and soothing voice. The young stallion's breathing slowed and its hooves took root. Its eyelids drooped, and when it sighed from deep within its chest, its nostrils fluttered in complete relaxation. Overhead, the crow, ignored and insulted, flew away squawking, its ebony wings gleaming in the thin winter sunlight.

Houston reined High Man up short. The old stallion blew hard and lowered its head. Its upper lip absently worried a few leaves and then it sighed. Behind them, the Thoroughbred mares trembled with exhaustion, sweat dripping from their flanks despite the chill of December. The mare in foal began to paw at the dead leaves underfoot, like something feral making a night's shelter.

"These horses need hay and grain," Dixie said in a weary, hopeless voice as she dismounted and checked her mare's sweat-soaked cinch. "They are about ready to drop, they're so weak."

Ruff and Houston just nodded, and the latter said, "We'll get them a feed tonight and a bed of straw if we can see our way out of this forest."

"We will," Ruff added, knowing that Dixie was deeply worried about the mares. It troubled him beyond words to see how thin the Ballou horses had become since fleeing Wildwood Farm and their beloved Tennessee. They looked to be down a few houndred pounds each.

A flash of movement caught the corner of Ruff's eye, and he spun on his heel, right hand stabbing downward, the Army Colt leaping upward and lining true against the flash of motion.

"Easy!" Houston ordered. "It was just a fox!"

Ruff closed his eyes and lowered the hammer of his Colt, for he'd also seen the fox an instant before he would have fired.

"You're almost too good with that six-gun," Houston said. "You've practiced the draw and shoot so much it's automatic. That kind of reaction can lead a man down the wrong trail."

"It can also keep him out of the grave," Dixie said, defending her favorite brother.

Houston turned away and Ruff made a show of checking his cinch. He appreciated Dixie coming to his defense, but he knew that Houston resented Dixie's obvious favoritism. It had never mattered when they were a large family, but now that it was just the three of them . . . well, Ruff meant to see that absolutely nothing came between their common bond and so he wished that Dixie would sometimes take Houston's part rather than his own.

Ruff leaned against High Fire for support and continued to examine everything in his range of vision. He had already decided that this forest was different from those back home in Tennessee. There were a few unfamiliar trees and oddly shaped ferns, even a few species of birds that Ruff had never seen before. The forest seemed runtier and drier, the sky not quite so blue. In truth, Ruff supposed he was not being very fair. All that he knew for certain was that he did not feel comfortable in this Arkansas forest and he longed for the Great Smoky Mountains and the beauty of the Cumberland Valley.

Tennessee. Would he ever return to Wildwood Farm to rebuild his father's great horse farm? Ruff was sure that it was now only a charred ruin trampled and desecrated by General Sherman's plundering army on its march to the sea. Besides their beloved horse farm, Ruff had lost three older brothers in the war, as well as his father, who had been shot down by a vicious Confederate lieutenant named Clemson Pike. Retribution had been swift, vengeance sweet. No one knew that the Confederate patrol had opened fire on the Ballous, forcing them to retaliate in self-defense. When the gun-smoke had cleared, Southerner had killed Southerner. And now, the Ballou name was a Southern curse and a Rebel was as much the enemy as a damned Yankee.

Just thinking about the loss of his father and his three older brothers brought a sharp ache to Ruff's throat. The Civil War had destroyed his world, his hopes, and his family's name. Gone was his boyhood dream of continuing to breed and race the finest horses in the South. Gone, too, was the thirty-some years of breeding records and effort that had produced stallions like High Man and his son, High Fire, the flashy three-year-old stallion Ruff now rode. Horses with the speed of Pegasus and the heart of Leo the Lion.

Ruff found it nearly impossible to turn his back on Tennessee and the South. He had nothing to go to out west except some Cherokee relatives on his mother's side of the family that he did not know. Tennessee was a part of him and it always would be. He longed for its great green forests, its sweet rivers, and its deep, placid ponds. Its forests were a hunter's paradise, with squirrels, coons, deer, and bears. Even a poor man with a good rifle could stay fat and content in Tennessee. Ruff did not think the same could be said of Arkansas.

But Tennessee was lost now. The entire South was on its knees while the armies of the North beat it senseless in a bloody rage of destruction. No Southerner—honored or dishonored—would be spared if he or she were caught fleeing with arms or property. As a defeated people, they were expected to beg for mercy and forgiveness. And so men still too proud to bend their neck or their knees were abandoning the South and heading west to start a new life.

Houston uncorked his canteen, drank deeply, and said, "We've seen two Yankee patrols on the river road in the last six hours. I'm afraid that if we don't keep to this forest we'll be spotted."

"We can't make any time if we never dare to use a road," Dixie argued.

Houston didn't seem to hear her. "Out west," he said, before taking another pull on his canteen, "I've heard there are vast stretches of grasslands and plains. Open country that rolls under a blue sky farther than our mere mortal imaginations can conceive. In that kind of country, you don't need roads. Not maps nor even directions."

Dixie's smudged but pretty face telegraphed her skepticism. "How do you figure?"

Houston frowned. "Out on the western plains, the sun is your daytime guide and your nightime compass is the North Star. Out there a might feels no more significant than a cork bobbing on the Atlantic Ocean, Dixie."

"It sounds awful!" Dixie screwed up her face. "With nothing but grass and sky, how do you hide from danger?"

"You don't hide," Houston said. "You fight—or you run—depending."

"I'd feel exposed without forest to hide in," Dixie said. "And I've heard the Sioux, the Kiowa, and those other tribes are a terror. If they catch you out in the open, you'd have no chance at all."

"Unless," Ruff said, "you're riding a Ballou Thoroughbred. In that case, you've nothing to worry about from some scrawny Indian pony."

"Who would we sell our horses to in the West?" Dixie demanded. "And who'd there be to race them against?"

When her older brothers failed to answer, she smirked. "See! Take my word for it, if we go too far west, we'll starve or get ourselves scalped."

"You are such an encouragement," Houston said cryptically. "What do you think, Ruff?"

"I miss Tennessee but I'm tired of war," he answered. "I've seen enough death to last me a lifetime. I want to raise, train, and race Ballou Thoroughbreds."

"Don't we all," Houston said, thumbing back his hat as his eyes roamed, restless and wary. He was the oldest surviving Ballou, just twenty-one but a blocky six-footer, solid and devilishly handsome. Under his right knee rested a Spencer Repeating Rifle, a prize taken from Lieutenant Pike.

Houston twisted all around in his saddle and made it clear that he was ready to travel again. "Shall we follow the river?"

Ruff scratched a place behind High Fire's ears and the stallion rubbed its sweaty head against Ruff's hip.

"If we do that, most likely we'll chance upon a patrol."

"Yeah," Houston agreed. "But we don't even know where the hell we are, much less where we can find our mother's Cherokee people."

"They're in these parts," Dixie said. "That's what Pa always claimed."

"No disrespect," Ruff replied, "but Pa hadn't visited these people in years, and we were so young the last time he brought us that all we remember is a big river."

"Has to be the Arkansas River yonder," Houston growled. "Seems to me we just need to find a little town and start asking questions."

Ruff knew that his brother was making sense, and yet most of the towns were under the control of the Union army. Every bit as dangerous and to be feared were the roving bands of deserters and opportunists looking to rob and kill. And even though the Ballou horses were thin and their coats dull and mud caked, anyone with even a rudimentary knowledge of horseflesh would realize at a glance that these Thoroughbreds were extremely valuable. All the Ballou horses tended toward sorrels, chestnuts with a few bays thrown in for good measure. Most of them had blazed faces, and a few, like High Fire, had four white stockings.

"We could just look for a little farm along the river to rest at," Dixie said. "We've got enough money to pay for what we need."

"That sounds good to me," Ruff said, plenty willing to avoid the towns and cities.

Houston, however, was of a different mind. "I don't know," he said with a frown. "I'd rather we checked things out. If we go to a farm, they might not be able to tell us much of anything. Might even lie and get us into trouble."

"Why would they do that?" Ruff questioned.

"Well, you just never know," Houston said. "I'm for going into a town and finding out everything we can about this part of the country. We don't know for sure that Mother's people are still in these parts. They might have left Arkansas for the Indian Territory. We could waste a lot of time going from one farm to another without really finding much out."

Ruff exchanged glances with Dixie. He could see that she was not won over by the argument, especially the part about some farmer turning them over to the Union army.

"Why don't we angle over to the river and follow it until we come onto something," Houston said in his most reasonable voice. "That's the time to make up our minds."

"These horses won't last another night without rest and feed," Dixie insisted.

Her warning wasn't really necessary, and since someone had to be in charge and since Houston was the eldest among them, Ruff decided to go along with his brother's suggestion. He and Dixie mounted, then lined out toward the big river they'd spotted from a hilltop not more than an hour before.

In less than twenty minutes, they came upon a good road overhung by enormous maple and elm trees, their naked branches cobwebbing the afternoon sky. From the looks of things, this was a busy road that followed the Arkansas River in a generally northwestern direction. The river itself wasn't anything to compare to the Mississippi, but it was impressive. "We'll find towns all along this one," Houston predicted even as a pair of freight wagons pulled by mules came rumbling into view.

The Ballous reined off to the side of the road until the wagons drew near, and then Houston rode High Man out and yelled, "Hello there!"

The driver of the first wagon was a ferret-faced little man whose cheek was bulging with tobacco. He spat a dark stream in Houston's direction and kept right on driving, spitting once more as he passed.

Houston's cheeks blazed with anger but he held his tongue until the second wagon approached, and then he rode directly into its path.

"Git out the way, you dern fool!" the driver shouted.

But Houston and High Man stood their ground and the sensible mules pulled up short.

"Git out the way!" the man screamed, raising a bullwhip.

In reply, Houston stubbornly clenched his jaw but then barked, "All I want is a little information."

"You'll get the lash of my whip if you don't move that horse!"

"Uh-oh," Dixie said. "Big trouble."

Ruff agreed because Houston had a fearsome temper. Ruff saw the first wagon come to a stop and the driver poking his weasel face around the corner, looking back. He spat tobacco juice and then vanished for an instant, only to reappear as he set his brake, then leaped to the road.

"Big trouble for sure," Ruff said, pushing his coat aside to reveal the butt of his Army Colt. "Dixie, you just stay with the horses and keep back out of the way of any bullets that might start flying."

"We can ask someone else about these parts!"

Ruff dismounted and offered his reins to Dixie. "Not very likely, seeing as how we both know Houston."

Houston reined his stallion off the road and around close to the driver with the bullwhip.

"You any good with that thing?" Ruff heard his brother ask the irate driver.

"You damn right I am! You cause me any grief and I'll hide you to the bone!"

"Oh yeah?" Houston's hand suddenly left his saddle horn to grab the bullwhip. With a powerful heave, he jerked the startled driver off his box, and the man crashed to the ground, swearing and thrashing.

Houston dismounted and tied High Man to the spokes of the wagon's wheel. All that time the driver was picking himself up off the ground and coiling his bullwhip. Before he could let it fly, however, Houston pivoted around on his heel and drove an uppercut from knee level that landed just below the driver's ribs.

Ruff saw the man with the bullwhip actually lift himself a couple of inches off the ground. Saw his cheeks balloon outward and his eyes bug. Saw the sick fear in his eyes as a curse died on his distended lips.

The tobacco spitter came to a halt about thirty feet from Houston and started to raise his rifle. There was a wicked grin on his face telling Ruff that the driver had killed before—and enjoyed it.

"Drop the rifle!" Ruff shouted, his hand dipping to the gun on his hip.

Ferret Face dropped, but not the rifle. Instead, he dived to the ground, rolled twice, and came up with his rifle swinging toward Ruff.

"Damn!" Ruff swore, squeezing his trigger. Blaze and black powder smoke exploded from the muzzle of his Army Colt. He heard the rifleman yelp in pain, but the wounded man still managed to unleash a ball at Ruff, who fired again.

The man collapsed in death. His mouth sagged open and a huge wad of tobacco slid wetly across his lips and onto his arm. The sight of the first driver completely unnerved the second, and he threw one hand up while the other held his aching gut.

"Don't kill me, ya tall bastards!" he screamed. "Don't kill me, now!"

Ruff glanced over at Dixie, who looked a bit pale. He shrugged as if to let her know that he had not wanted to kill the mule skinner but the fool had given him no other choice.

"Have mercy!" the second driver cried as Houston dragged him to his feet and slammed him up against one of his mules. "Have mercy! I got a wife and kids!"

Houston's fist had been cocked and his eyes were wild with fury. "None of this would have been necessary if either one of you jackasses would have been even half-civil!"

The driver's mouth worked silently. "You don't know, mister," he wheezed. "You just don't know."

"Don't know what?"

"There's all kinds of sons a bitches on the roads these days. We got orders never to stop, talk, or do nothin' except keep these wagons moving."

"All we needed was a little local advice on these parts," Houston growled. "And now you've gone and got your pardner shot."

"He wasn't worth much," the driver rationalized. "He was really ornerier than hell. But I don't know what I'm going to do with his wagon."

"You drive it on the to the next town," Ruff said. "Mules are real smart. One team will most likely follow the other home."

"You think so?"

"I'm almost sure of it."

The driver looked very relieved, but then he frowned and said, "I'd appreciate it if you'd come along and explain to the boss how come you had to shoot Bob."

"Sorry," Ruff said, "but we're sort of in a hurry. How far up the road is the next town?"

"That'd be Hadley. About six miles."

Houston interrupted. "Is it in Union hands?"

"Of course. All of this country hereabouts is."

"That's what we were afraid of," Houston said, then added quickly, "You ever heard of a family around here called Starr?"

"Nope, and I know most everyone."

"They're Cherokee," Dixie explained.

The man scowled. "We already run most of them sons a bitches out of Arkansas a long while back. Probably be over in the Indian Territory if they ain't dead."

The skin tightened around the corners of Houston's eyes but he held his tongue and turned on his heel.

"Hey!" the driver called. "Won't you at least help me lift Bob up into the wagon!"

Ruff was seething from the slur about his mother's people, and he knew that the best thing he could do right now was to get moving, so he touched his heels to the flanks of High Fire and they headed up the road toward a town called Hadley.

Ruff did not know what they might do next. He was sure that they would create a lot of attention when they arrived, and if word got back about the driver they'd just shot, someone might even be fool enough to attempt an arrest.

"I think we'd better hunt us up a prosperous-looking farm in this neighborhood," Ruff said to his brother and sister.

"Agreed," Dixie replied.

But Houston looked straight ahead down the road with the kind of faraway look in his eye that told Ruff his brother was probably thinking of a Confederate spy he'd fallen in love with named Molly O'Day. Molly had gone north to Washington, D.C., and even though almost a month had passed, Houston had still not quite gotten over his disappointment.

"Houston?"

"What?"

"You thinking about Molly O'Day again?"

"Yeah."

"Molly will probably find you someday," Ruff said, trying to boost his brother's low spirits.

Houston sighed. "Ruff, the world is full of beautiful young women. Without half trying, a couple of good-looking men like ourselves can find them in droves."

"Ha!" Dixie said, twisting around in the saddle to watch the driver they'd left behind hoist Bob's corpse into the second freight wagon.

"Well, it's true enough," Houston said, trying to convince himself of his own words.

Ruff didn't say anything. He wasn't ugly but he was a long way from being handsome by any definition. And getting most of his right earlobe shot off in the war hadn't done a thing for his appearance, either. His black hair was long enough to cover the disfigurement, but when he shook his head or the wind blew, the missing earlobe was plain for anyone to see. His father had once had a mare with the top of one ear bit off by a stallion. It had bothered old Justin so much he'd sold the mare rather than have it at Wildwood. When Ruff had asked his father about that, Justin had replied that he wouldn't have a mare that might throw one-eared colts. The old man had tried to make a joke, but failed.

Either way, it was Ruff's considered opinion that one-eyed or one-eared things bothered some folks and that no pretty girl would give such a disfigured fella as himself even a second glance unless she was also missing something.

TWO

Late that afternoon, they met a carriage, and its driver introduced himself as Mr. Thompson. He was a large, ruddy-faced gentleman of obvious means with a gold pocket watch, a silvery bush of beard, and a hearty laugh.

"Sure, I remember the Starrs," he said, nodding his double chins. "They were good people and they lived all over these parts. But most all of them relocated to the Indian Territory ten, fifteen years ago."

"You said 'most all of them,'" Houston replied. "Does that mean a few remain in Arkansas?"

"There are still Cherokee in these parts. Not many. Most lost their property or had it taken. The full-bloods still look and act like Indians. They are dark and they wear Indian clothes. We don't have much use for them in these parts. But the mixed-bloods, well, they all have English and French names and so much white blood in their veins that you couldn't tell them from a white."

"We're part Cherokee," Ruff said, eyes boring into the man to gauge his reaction.

There was a long moment of awkward silence, then Thompson said, "Well, if I were you folks, I'd just keep that little fact to yourselves. Folks in these parts tolerate Indians, but most won't lift a hand to help them. And the Cherokee that were left alone hereabouts are the ones that had enough money and sense not to advertise being part Indian."

Thompson drew a long cigar from out of his pocket, cut the tip off with a little silver knife, and lit it. He smoked for a minute before he regarded the Ballou Thoroughbreds.

"You people got some fine-looking horses. You interested in selling 'em?"

"No," Houston said. "But we are interested in finding them a barn and a good feed of hay and grain."

The friendliness died in the man's eyes. "Sorry, can't help you. These are hard, hard times."

"We were hoping to find my mother's people," Dixie explained. "Her name was Lucinda Eldee Starr."

The heavyset man raised his bushy eyebrows. "Well, I'll be! There's a big family of Eldee people just up the road about three miles. You can't miss their farm on the right. One of the best in this part of Arkansas."

Dixie sighed with relief. "Good. We'll pay them a visit, that's for sure."

Thompson shook his head. "Me and my family have never socialized with the Eldees. They've always kept to themselves. Never even joined the Baptist Church in Hadley. I guess no one ever realized they were a pack of Cherokees."

Ruff didn't want to cause the Eldees any trouble. "They're probably not, Mr. Thompson. Most likely, Eldee is an English name and those people haven't a drop of Indian blood."

"Well, you just never know," Thompson said, his brow furrowing. "They might be Cherokee."

Dixie's cheeks flamed but before she vented her anger, Ruff and Houston grabbed her reins, tipped their hats, and continued on down the road.

"I can't believe my ears!" Dixie stormed. "You damn near apologized for the fact that there might be some Indian blood in the Eldee line!"

"Don't you get it?" Houston snapped. "The only reason that the Eldees and a few other mixed-blood Cherokee have been allowed to remain in this part of Arkansas is that they've kept quiet about their Indian blood. My guess is that this family doesn't look any more Indian than we do—which isn't very much."

Dixie's face grew pinched. "It's wrong when anyone has to hide their ancestry."

"Of course it is," Ruff said, "but if they chose to do it,

then that's *their* right. As it is, we've probably raised a doubt in Mr. Thompson's mind and he'll most likely express that doubt to others. Could be we just created a big problem for the Eldee family."

Dixie's anger evaporated. "I didn't mean that we should put anyone in a bad position. That wasn't what I meant at all."

"We know that," Ruff said. "But I sensed that despite how outwardly friendly Mr. Thompson was, he harbored some prejudice against the Cherokee."

Dixie twisted in her saddle to look at the departing buggy but her head snapped around an instant later.

"What?" Ruff asked, sensing Dixie's alarm.

"Mr. Thompson. Our eyes just met and . . . well, he had the strangest look on his face. He wasn't smiling anymore."

Ruff shook his head hoping that they had not inadvertently caused the Eldees any harm. He guessed things were different in Arkansas because back in Tennessee people hadn't cared if his family claimed Cherokee blood. Maybe that was because his father, Justin Ballou, was mostly French and Irish, and his half-Cherokee mother had died years before while off in the Smoky Mountains helping her people during a cholera epidemic.

Maybe. But maybe, too, things were going to be different out in the West. Different enough that having Indian blood might generally be held against a person. Ruff expelled a deep breath. As if their being branded traitors to the South because they'd had no choice but to defend themselves against a Conferate patrol wasn't enough of a burden to carry, now there was this Indian thing to weigh him down.

"I remember," Houston said, "that Mother once tried to explain to me how her people had suffered when they'd been relocated from the eastern forests to the West. She said thousands of Cherokee died on the Trail of Tears."

Ruff had heard of the Trail of Tears many times. It was, however, something that wasn't talked about much among whites because it was so shameful. And it was Ruff's observation that shame and silence were common bedfellows.

"That looks like it might be the Eldee farm up ahead," Houston said as they rode over a low hilltop and gazed down at a small valley neatly divided into pastures and paddocks.

Ruff could see at a glance that the Eldees had prospered despite a war that had devastated most of the South. True, the pastures were empty except for a few milk cows, mules, and workhorses. Closer inspection, however, showed that the farmhouse, barn, and fences were in good repair and freshly painted. The weeds under the fence lines were chopped down, the gravel that covered a big circular driveway was raked, and the flower gardens were well tended. There were very few farms left in the South that still retained this kind of pride or polish.

"What do you think?" Houston asked.

"I hope they're friendly," Dixie said. "These mares are about to quit."

"Then let's go see if these folks are related to Mother," Houston said.

As they rode up the lane toward the farmhouse, Ruff felt a rising sense of excitement. If these really were his mother's side of the family, then he might learn new things about her past. Ruff's father, God rest his soul, had been incapable of talking about Lucinda Eldee Starr except in painful reminiscences. He'd speak of Lucinda in a distant way, maybe recalling something they had done together. Some incident that had stuck in his mind for one reason or another. Often, it was how they'd met at a horse race, or of the time they'd traveled to Washington, D.C., with a group of Cherokee led by the famed Sam Houston to plead for Indian land and justice.

As they neared the farmhouse an old man and his wife, along with a woman of about forty and a girl about Ruff's age, appeared. All but the girl were very light skinned.

Ruff and Houston both removed their hats as they reined in their played-out horses, with Dixie and the mares pressed in behind. It was not considered proper to dismount until invited, so they remained in their saddles.

"Good evening," Houston said, addressing the old man and

woman. "Sorry to have bothered you this fine day."

The old man was wasted with pain and sickness. He stared at the sound of Houston's voice rather than at Houston himself and it quickly became evident he was blind. His wife also seemed to be in frail health but her eyes were clear, not cloudy.

"Evening," replied the middle-aged woman without any warmth in her greeting.

The Ballous waited in vain to be invited to dismount. Houston, who was better at words than Ruff, shifted uncomfortably in his saddle. The woman's dark eyes held no warmth and no greeting. She was hollow cheeked and clutched at a gray shawl wrapped around her thin shoulders. Her dress was clean but faded, and under it poked round-toed and scuffed work boots.

After almost a minute of silence, Houston worked up a smile and said, "This is a fine place you folks have. Very nice. We had a place like this in Tennessee called Wildwood Farm. We raised the finest Thoroughbred racehorses in the South. Maybe you've heard of it?"

"No," the woman said, pressing her arms tight against her flat chest. She did not even bother to look at the Thoroughbreds. "We don't get about much. We like to stay to ourselves."

"I understand," Houston said, eyes shifting to the older couple, then back to the woman. "We were pretty settled ourselves until the war. Lost our father and three brothers in the service of the South. Father's name was Justin. Justin Ballou. Our brothers were John, Micha, and Mason. They all died on the battlefield—except Pa."

When neither the woman or the old couple displayed any sympathy or interest, Houston said, "Does the name Ballou mean anything to you folks?"

"Not a thing," the woman replied.

"What about Starr?"

The woman licked her thin, withered lips. She wrung her hands together, and Ruff felt a twinge of pity for her because she looked so hard used. Her hair was streaked with dirty gray and pulled back in a severe bun that made her ears appear too large and her neck too skinny. She wore no jewelry or even a hint of color and, if Ruff had to guess, she had also seen her share of sorrow due to the war. Maybe it had not destroyed this farm, but Ruff could see that it had touched the woman because of the pain in her eyes.

"Mister," the woman said, "my family is setting down to supper and unless you've got something better to do than ask questions, turn those horses around and ride."

Ruff started to lift his reins but Dixie said, "Our horses are about to drop, ma'am. We have money and we'd be grateful if you'd let us board them in your barn tonight. We'll pay for their feed and . . ."

"That is out of the question."

"But why!" Dixie demanded. "We'll sleep in the barn with the horses and cause neither you nor your family any trouble."

"Strangers," the woman said, "are always trouble. Please go."

The woman slipped her hand through the crook of the old lady's arm and started to turn, but Ruff said, "Does the name Eldee mean anything to you?"

The thin, weary woman froze, then turned back to face Ruff. Her expression had turned wary. "We're Eldee people. Everyone knows that."

"Our mother's name was Lucinda Eldee Starr. She had people that left North Carolina and came here for a time. They were mixed-blood Cherokee."

"We're *white* folks!" the woman said angrily. "Now ride off this property!"

The young woman Ruff's age took a step forward and Ruff could see that she was upset and trying to hold her tongue. Their eyes met and stuck. Ruff's cheeks suddenly warmed. Her eyes were like pools of quicksand, seeming to pull him into their depths. Ruff gulped and tried to say something to her but he was at a complete loss for words. He was strangely incapable of anything more than to work his mouth in the silence. Like an idiot.

"Ruff?" It was Dixie.

He stopped trying to speak and made an effort to at least smile at the young woman. Her complexion was olive and, if he were to guess, he would have thought her part Cherokee, for she had the same look as the old daguerreotypes he'd seen of his mother. Her face was heart shaped, her forehead broad, and her nose straight. Her lips were full, her eyes . . . well, they could bore through a man and read the tracks of his wandering mind. Her figure was willowy and small waisted. Like Dixie, she was tall, with hair the color of a raven's wing.

"I'm a Starr," the young woman announced. "And my mother was related to your mother. In fact, I believe they were first cousins."

"Thia!" the middle-aged woman cried. "These people must leave at once!"

The girl ignored her. She spoke to Ruff in a very controlled, tense voice. "I have heard of Wildwood Farm and of these racehorses."

"Thia, that's enough!"

"Let her be, Margaret," the old woman interrupted, speaking for the first time. Head shaking with palsy, she turned to the young woman. "Thia, this is still Mr. Eldee's and my farm. You invite these people to put their horses in our barn, then come inside and take supper."

The woman who had told Ruff to leave stomped to the porch with the heel of her work boot, then whirled and marched into the house.

The old blind man started to cackle, then he began to choke. He had to be helped to a chair on the porch. As soon as he caught his breath, he started giggling, head down, cloudy eyes tied to the floor. It was then that Ruff realized the old man was not only blind, he was deranged.

The young woman named Thia said, "Please excuse Aunt Margaret. She had a very bad experience with some Confederate deserters nearly a year ago. She no longer trusts strangers."

Dixie saved Ruff from saying something stupid. "I guess

if we're distant cousins, we ought to introduce ourselves."

After the introductions were made, Thia led them to the barn, and their exhausted Thoroughbreds were unsaddled and fed.

"If you don't come in for supper pretty soon, it'll all be cold," Thia said, sitting on a bucket and watching as the three Ballous curried their horses.

"We've got some food in our saddlebags," Ruff said. "I think it would better if we ate here with the horses tonight. No use upsetting Aunt Margaret."

"She's been upset ever since she lost Uncle Leo at Shiloh."

"That's where we lost our brother, Micha," Houston said. "And John went down at Bull Run."

"Everyone has lost someone," Thia told them. "Like you, I have lost brothers."

"In which battles?" Houston asked.

Thia looked right through him. "I lost them not to battles, but to bigotry. You see, Mr. Ballou, the Starrs are half-bloods, but I side with the full-bloods—to Aunt Margaret's disgust—and prefer to hang on to the old Indian customs and culture. For this, we are persecuted just as Indians everywhere are persecuted."

Houston looked very uncomfortable. "We're just horsemen, Miss Starr. I meant no disrespect or anything. I figured that your brothers must have fought for the South and been killed, that's all."

"They, like most of the full-bloods, tried to stay out of the war. We tried to be neutral, but that was impossible. The mix-bloods owned slaves, so they went with the South. Some of the full-bloods chose the North because they did not believe in owning slaves. There was fighting even between us. Here, and in the Indian Territory."

"Are the Starrs in Oklahoma?"

Thia nodded. "Most of them that have survived. And the Eldees as well."

"Why . . . never mind," Dixie said, "it's none of my business."

The hardness smoothed out of Thia's lovely face. "What were you about to ask?"

"I wanted to know why you stayed here if most all of your family left for the Indian Territory."

"I take care of my grandparents and this place," Thia said. "But Aunt Margaret and I fight too much now. I think I will leave."

"To go to the Indian Territory?" Ruff asked.

"Where else for someone like me?"

The question caught Ruff by surprise. "Why . . . why you could go anywhere you wanted."

"A Cherokee woman?" Thia looked through Ruff's eyes with a patient smile on her lips. "Mr. Ballou," she said, "you have much to learn."

He blushed and was about to say something when a young Negro appeared at the barn door. "Mrs. Eldee, she say you better come along if'n you and these folk gonna eat, Miss Thia."

"We'll be right along, George." Thia turned to them. "Your fine horses are getting a good feed, now you need to eat yourselves. You're almost as thin as your Thoroughbreds."

Houston, Dixie, and Ruff exchanged glances before Houston said, "Let's put them in the stalls and go eat. I'm so hungry my backbone is rubbing against my breastbone."

Ruff wasn't of a mind to object. He was famished and he knew that Dixie was, too. When they entered the house, Thia led them along a dim hallway into a dining room. The old folks were not present, but Aunt Margaret was waiting, seated at the head of the table, and she glared at them.

"Be seated."

They took their seats, and without any prayer or preamble, plates of roast pork, potatoes, and corn on the cob were served by a Negro woman.

Houston was too hungry to hold his appetite in check. He filled his plate and sawed a slab of pork from the roast, which he shoved into his mouth.

"Delicious, Mrs. Eldee," he said around a mouthful of food.

Ruff and Dixie mumbled something of the same, and their mother would have been mortified at the way they devoured the meal. They ate seconds and then thirds, and no one declined the chocolate cake that was served for dessert.

"Well," Margaret said when her guests were finally satisfied and looking a little sheepish because of their poor table manners. "So you are Lucinda's offspring."

"Yes, ma'am," Houston said, accepting a cigar from a silver humidor. "As you probably know, our mother died seven years ago among the Cherokee in the Great Smoky Mountains."

"I didn't know your mother all that well," Margaret said. "We were raised quite differently. And of course, she went with the Confederacy."

Ruff almost dropped his coffee cup. "And you didn't?"

"I sided with no one!" Margaret snapped. "It was especially stupid of any Cherokee to side with the Confederacy."

"Why?" Houston demanded.

"Because, in doing so, Chief Ross and the other tribal leaders forfeited more than five million dollars that was supposed to be paid by the United States government to the Cherokee for lands the Indians gave up in North Carolina, Georgia, and Tennessee. Five million dollars!"

"But we *are* Southerners!" Dixie cried. "Would you have us side with the North!"

"I'd have us side with victory!" Margaret challenged. "Instead, we pledged ourselves to Jefferson Davis, and look what ruin it's brought! Haven't the Cherokee suffered enough without allowing themselves to be dragged into the loser's side of the war! When are we going to use our heads and save what we have left instead of fighting battles that cannot be won!"

Thia flushed deeply with anger. She threw her napkin down on the table and managed to say, "Excuse me," before she hurried outside.

The young woman left a strained silence in her wake. Finally, Margaret said, in a weary voice, "Thia is young and idealistic. She hasn't lost a husband. She isn't old enough to remember the relocation that our people went through twenty-five years ago. She thinks she knows hardship, but she doesn't really."

"She lost brothers," Ruff said in a tight voice. "That's hardship."

"Yes, it is. They were killed while raiding with that fool, Stand Watie and his First Cherokee Mounted Rifles."

"They're a proud fighting unit," Houston said, barely able to conceal his Southern indignation.

"Oh, they're brave, all right," Margaret clipped. "And Stand Watie is no fool. He's made himself quite a reputation, and folks say he will soon earn himself the rank of brigadier general. Most Cherokee think he's some great hero."

Margaret's voice trembled and she shook her finger at them. "I tell you this, Stand Watie will earn the Cherokee people nothing but heartache. The federal government will judge us all by his so-called heroics and for that we'll suffer long after this terrible war is over."

Houston bounced to his feet and it was all he could do to say, "I don't see much 'suffering' here, Mrs. Eldee. I see a farm that has been spared the devastation of the South. I see Negro servants, horses, and well-tended lawns and fields. I think I also see a turncoat."

"Houston!" Ruff thundered.

"It's true! Look at this place!" He jabbed a finger at Margaret Eldee. "I'm asking you how you've managed to avoid the devastation that the rest of us Southerners have endured."

The woman paled and began to shake. Finally, her lips moved across clenched front teeth. "Get the hell out of my house and off my land! All of you!"

Dixie pushed back in her chair so violently that she spilled over onto the carpet. Humiliated and furious, she jumped to her feet and ran for the front door, and Houston stomped out right behind her.

Only Ruff remained calm enough to speak. "You *are* a turncoat, Mrs. Eldee. You've traded honor for comfort. Respect for your own Indian heritage."

"I've traded a husband and sons for a house and land!" she cried. "I've traded precious, wasted blood for reason!"

Ruff twisted his hat in his hand. Unlike the others, he felt no anger toward this woman, only pity. "Our Thoroughbreds are played out the same as we are," he said, reaching into his pocket for a wad of Confederate money. "We can't go on without them resting a day or two."

"Save that worthless paper," Margaret said bitterly. "When you get to the Indian Territory and you settle on the reservation, use it to chink the walls in your cabin. Or to start a fire on your hearth. Or better yet, give it to General Watie and tell him to use it to wipe himself."

Ruff blushed and headed for the door. He stopped before leaving, turned, and said, "Mrs. Eldee, I don't believe you are much of a lady."

"No more than you, sir, are an Indian."

THREE

That night, a storm swept across Arkansas. The temperature plunged, and Ruff awoke to hear the wind whining through the cedar, birch, and hickory trees that surrounded the barn. Before falling asleep, Ruff had left a lantern burning, and now it flickered in the wind sifting through the wall cracks.

Ruff walked over to the lantern and lifted it as he moved down the line of stalls. High Man and High Dancer were still eating. The mares were alert but not alarmed. Even so, Ruff went inside each stall and rubbed each mare behind the ears, speaking the nonsensical horse talk for which his family was renowned back in Tennessee.

It was frigid in the barn, but clouds of warm breath pulsated in and out of the horses' nostrils. But the animals were content and no longer hungry. Back at Wildwood, the mares would have been blanketed in their stalls, but that was impossible here.

"Are they all right?" Dixie asked, startling Ruff.

"Yeah, they're fine," he said, closing a stall door. "It's a good thing that we are inside tonight. It would have been pretty miserable sleeping out in the woods."

Dixie nodded. She looked tired and there were dark shadows around her eyes. "What are we going to do about tomorrow?"

"I don't know," Ruff confessed. "We can't stay here if we're not wanted."

"Yes, we can," Dixie said. "And like it or not, that woman is our distant relative. What kind of a person would turn their

25

own kinfolk out in a winter storm?"

"A bitter woman."

"I'll tell her we're staying even if you won't," Dixie said. "These horses aren't fit to travel in this bitter weather. Not in their poor condition."

Ruff knew that Dixie was right. If they attempted to travel and the storm intensified, they'd lose mares to pneumonia. "If this storm doesn't pass come morning, we can *both* tell her," Ruff said wearily. "These mares aren't fit to buck through snow. If we leave, we'll just have to find shelter all over again."

"I was talking to Thia last night after you and Houston went to sleep."

"She came in here?"

"No. I went outside to look at the stars and I saw her sitting on the porch all alone. So I went over and we talked. She's coming with us to the Indian Territory."

Ruff frowned. "I'm not sure that's such a good idea. Remember, we're wanted by both the Union and Confederacy. There might even be a bounty on our heads."

"Pssh-wash!" Dixie snorted. "The Confederacy is dying. Its money is worthless. What are they going to offer a bounty with?"

Dixie didn't expect an answer and she pushed on. "And as for the North, what have we done to them?"

"Houston and I killed more than a few over by Lookout Mountain. That's when I lost my earlobe, remember?"

"Oh well," Dixie said, dismissing this fact as having no merit whatsoever, "everyone knows there was a war going on and both sides fought for what they believed in. My point is that we aren't anything special in the eyes of the Union army."

"Maybe not," Ruff said, "but if they catch us with these horses, they'll want them, and we'll have to fight."

"Then we just won't get caught," Dixie said. "Besides, Thia told me that she knows all the back roads leading to the Indian Territory. She can keep us away from any Union patrols and get us safely to Oklahoma. And once there, we can find the Starr families and settle down."

Ruff scowled and toed the dirt.

"What's the matter?"

"Dixie, we're only a quarter Cherokee. I'm not sure that I'm willing to have the government confine me to some reservation. We've never lived like Indians and are ignorant of Cherokee ways."

"Thia will help us make friends," Dixie said. "She's already said so. She's a half-blood and the full-bloods treat her like one of their own. She says that we'll be welcomed the same as if we were full-bloods."

Ruff walked over to the barn door. He handed the lantern to Dixie, then unbarred the door and opened it a crack. The wind caught the door and yanked him off his feet. Swirling snow spun into the barn and snuffed out the lantern. It took a few panicky moments to get the barn door closed and barred, then the lantern relit.

"What'd you do a dumb thing like that for?" Dixie demanded.

"I just wanted to see if the snow was sticking on the ground."

"Well, of course it was."

"I just wanted to see for myself."

Dixie shivered and batted away the snow that had covered her like a thin cloak. She wasn't pleased. "That doesn't make any sense to me at all!"

"A lot of things I do don't make sense," Ruff said, stomping back to his bedroll in a pile of straw.

Dixie set the lantern down in the middle of the floor on dirt. She came over to lie down beside Ruff, and then pulled her own blankets tightly around her.

Ruff closed his eyes and listened to the wind howl. Dixie was right, it had been a dumb thing to open the barn door.

"Ruff?"

"Go to sleep."

"Thia wanted to know about you."

Ruff's eyes popped open. "What do you mean 'know about me'?"

"Just what I said. She wanted to know how old you were, what you liked to do. If you had a girl back home. You know, that sort of personal stuff."

"Why?"

" 'Cause she liked the looks of you, rat-bit earlobe and all."

Ruff's cheeks blew out. He chuckled and fluttered his lips like a horse to let Dixie know that he thought this was not worth losing sleep over.

"You can snort all you want, Rufus Ballou, but I saw the way you stared at Thia! How you couldn't even speak when she looked you dead in the eye. You looked ready to swoon!"

Ruff snorted again so Dixie reached over in the dark and pounded him on the shoulder. "You act as if you had girls stashed away all over the South pining for the sight of you like we've seen 'em do for Houston. But I know different."

"Dixie, you talk way too damn much."

"I say things you don't want to hear."

"Go back to sleep. It's still a couple of hours before sunrise."

"Won't be any sunrise in a snowstorm," Dixie said. She yawned. "I sure wish I had a big warm dog to sleep with and keep me warm tonight."

"Go to sleep!"

"Or a big warm man."

"Dixie!"

She giggled. Snuggled down in her blankets and very soon, Ruff heard her even breathing under the sound of the wild wind outside. He turned and studied her profile in the dim lamplight. He remembered his father once saying that Dixie was going to look very much like her mother though she had a more difficult temperament and was far more outspoken and contentious.

Dixie *was* contentious, all right. She wasn't ever afraid to say exactly what was on her mind. But she was smart, quick, and brave. She'd stood with them during the fight where they'd had to kill their fellow Confederates rather than to allow them to confiscate the last of their Ballou Thoroughbreds to be used as cannon fodder on the battlefield. She also had a pretty accurate way of reading people, and Ruff relied on her judgment because he knew he was inclined to be far too trusting in most cases.

Ruff pulled Dixie's blanket up under her chin. He guessed that he loved Dixie more than anyone in the world. Even Houston.

Early the next morning, the barn door wedged open and Thia squeezed inside. She looked happy and alert.

"It stopped snowing just before dawn."

"How deep is it?" Ruff asked, still half-asleep.

"Only about a foot. But it ought to melt away by noon. Hungry?"

"Yes, but . . ."

"Good!" Thia reached back through the doorway and hauled in a basket of food and a jug of steaming black coffee, complete with enough cups to go around.

Houston sat up and used his long fingers to comb the straw out of his hair. "Good morning, Miss Eldee."

"Good morning, Houston."

He knuckled sleep out of his eyes and then spotted the snow wherever it had filtered through the wall cracks. "Did we get a storm?"

"We got a storm," Thia said brightly as she handed them each a cup and then poured them coffee. "A real good one, too. But the sky is as clean and clear as rain. It's cold out but it'll warm up soon enough."

Ruff sipped his coffee, unable to take his eyes off the young woman. She had long, brown fingers and lovely hands. They were supple and graceful, more so than Houston's, who had the handsomest hands Ruff had ever seen on anyone— male or female.

"This is real service," Houston said as he took a blueberry sweet roll from the plate Thia offered.

"Enjoy it," Thia said. "We've got some hard traveling to do today."

"Uh-uh," Dixie said. "Not in a foot of snow with these tired mares."

"But why not?"

"They're not up to it," Dixie explained. "We could push on for a few miles, but that's all. Frankly, Ruff and I have about decided to talk to your aunt and see if she will let us—"

"She won't," Thia said. "We've already said our good-byes this morning. She said she'd turn you into the Federals if they came by today."

Ruff found that hard to believe. "She'd really do that?"

Thia nodded, then shot an accusing glance at Houston. "You called her a turncoat and she's so angry that she says she'll be one if you don't leave."

Houston flushed. "Well, wasn't she anyway?"

"No."

"Then how—"

Thia cut him off. "A shot-up Union patrol came by several years ago. They'd been ambushed by the Rebs and they were on the run. If Aunt Margaret's husband had been here, there would have been more killing. But the menfolk were gone so we took the Union boys into the house and bandaged them up. We even dug a bullet out of one of them and he lived. Since then we've been treated with respect. It's only the deserters—both gray and blue—that we fear."

Houston climbed to his feet. "I'll go up to the house and apologize if your aunt will listen."

"She won't," Thia said. "And anyway, I told her that you'd feel like seven kind of a fool when you learned the truth about what happened here. She said you can stay a few more days but I said that might not be such a good idea."

"Why?"

"Because Union patrols often stop in to water their horses and take a snack. We feed them cookies and such."

Thia sighed. "They look so hungry and then they're so grateful. I can't say that I blame my aunt."

Houston rose and stretched, then walked over to look after the horses. "Ruff?"

"What?"

"Was this mare down all night?"

Ruff heard the undertone of concern in Houston's voice. He and Dixie rushed over to the stall, bringing the lantern. Houston was already in the stall, kneeling by the mare's side. The mare's name was High Ma'am and she was one of the older and weaker mares.

Ruff came in and knelt beside Houston. He bent over and placed his ear against the mare's ribs and listened. Her breathing was congested. It sounded labored. He looked into the mare's large brown eyes.

"Dixie, hold the lantern up high," Ruff said.

"I'll do it," Thia said, "I'm taller."

Ruff studied the mare's eyes and they seemed very bright. He ran his hand over her muzzle. It was dry and hot.

"She's running a temperature," Ruff said. "She's in trouble."

He looked at Dixie. "Your aunt and grandparents have horses and mules here. Do they keep any medicines around?"

"In the house."

"Do you think . . . ?"

"I'll bring whatever I can find."

"Good."

Thia started to turn and race off to the house but then she stopped, whirled, and called, "Ruff, do you think she'll pull through?"

He looked up at Thia, her face bathed in lamplight and filled with concern. "I think so," he said, bending over again to listen to the the mare's labored breathing and pressing his palm against her stomach to see if she was experiencing any abdominal pain.

The mare did not grunt with pain but sighed and closed its eyes. Ruff ran his hands over her barrel, feeling ribs and thinking about how fat and sleek she had been when they'd left Tennessee and by comparison how poor she looked now.

"How old is she, Dixie?"

"Older than I am."

"That's what I thought."

Houston said, "I'd guess she was about eighteen. Maybe even twenty. She's been with us since my earliest memory."

Ruff nodded. This mare had thrown some very fine colts and fillies. Some of her get had already had successful racing careers. When Ruff had been a barefoot boy, she had been his favorite riding mare. They'd spent many a happy day trotting over the countryside, grazing in lush meadows, splashing happily through streams.

"She's going to be all right," he said out loud to himself as he stroked the mare's rough coat. "Ain't right that she should die looking so poor and in a strange place."

Thia hurried back into the barn. She was slightly out of breath and Margaret was close behind.

"Here," Thia said, extending a large bottle of some kind of dark, syrupy elixir, "this is all we have."

Ruff studied the label, but it was covered with elixir and indecipherable. "What is it?"

"It's for coughs and fever," Margaret said, folding her arms across her chest and trying to look stern. "I never used it but my husband used to swear by it. Bought it by the gallon and said it worked."

Ruff shook the bottle. The medicine smelled of alcohol and something else that Ruff could not define. Maybe licorice with a little sage. Mostly, though, it was probably pure corn liquor with enough boosters to give it its own particular taste, look, and smell. That was the way with these frontier medicines, be they for man or beast.

"All right," Ruff said, motioning for Houston to kneel down beside him. "Lift and turn her head."

Houston had done this since he was a boy, and when the head was lifted and turned, Ruff reached in behind the big back teeth and grabbed the mare's tongue. He twisted it out and to the side, then jammed the bottle in and poured.

The old mare was so weak that she just swallowed, eyes rolling back in her head. Ruff gave her the entire bottle, half expecting Mrs. Eldee to scold him. He didn't care. The longer he looked at this mare the more he was convinced that she was in desperate shape. She should have struggled a lot more but was just too damned weak.

"All right," Ruff said, tossing the bottle aside and releasing the tongue to stroke the mare's throat. "Let her head down, Houston."

The mare sighed and closed her eyes. Dixie and Ruff exchanged glances, and Ruff could see that Dixie was also very worried.

"Mrs. Eldee," Houston said, "this mare is too sick to travel. She's old and worn down to nothing. We can leave her behind or—"

"No," the pinch-faced woman said, eyes fixed on the old mare, "I wouldn't know how to help her, so you just stay here until she either dies or gets strong enough to travel."

"That could be up to a week," Ruff said. "Maybe even longer."

"I'm aware of that." Margaret picked up her skirts and said, "I expect you to pay for your room and board—kin or no kin. Times are bad here, and I can't afford to feed you and all your horses for nothing."

"Like we've already told you, ma'am, all we've got is Confederate money," Ruff said. "And you told us what Jefferson Davis could do with that."

Ruff could have sworn the severe expression on Margaret's face eased a little before she said, "You can leave one of those younger mares that are in foal. I can sell a good horse."

"No!" Dixie cried. "We've only a few left and—"

"Dixie!" Houston's voice was harsh and commanding. "We'll do as the woman says. We have no choice."

"Sure we do!" Dixie turned to the woman. "Don't the fact that were are blood relatives mean *anything* to you?"

"You're trouble," Margaret said. "Pure and simple you are trouble if a Union patrol comes by for a visit and they find you in hiding."

"Any reason why they would come into this barn?" Houston asked.

"No."

"Then I don't see you have much to worry about. We'll keep the horses inside at all times. We'll pretty much stay in here as well during the daytime. It'll be all right, Mrs. Eldee."

The woman brushed a shaky hand across her eyes. She looked down at the old mare. "I hope she lives. Otherwise, we'll have to figure out a way to drag her off into the woods. Ground is too hard to dig a hole big enough to bury her."

Ruff bristled until Margaret knelt down and ran her pale, skinny fingers along the mare's neck. "I remember it said that your mother was a fine horsewoman. I expect that's where you got some of your own way with 'em. It wasn't all through your father, you know. The Starrs and Eldees always had fine horses."

"Yes, ma'am," Ruff said.

Margaret rose and looked at Thia. Something passed between the two, and Ruff hoped it was forgiveness and understanding. He could see that they'd shared some hard, uncompromising words. He knew from what Dixie had told him that Thia and Margaret had little use for each other and that their ideas about the role of the Cherokee people were diametrically opposed. Thia favored the full-blood, traditional way of life; Margaret seemed to want to divorce herself from all that was Indian about her and her past.

"I guess you'll be staying then for a while," Margaret said to the girl.

"I guess I will."

"Your grandpa and grandma will be pleased."

"I know."

Margaret turned. "I'll go tell them you'll be staying, then."

"All right."

When the woman disappeared, Thia knelt down beside Ruff and the mare. "Do you think the medicine will help?"

"Sure it will," Ruff said, not at all sure. "It would help if the weather warms up."

"We've got some blankets in the house. I'll bring them out and cover her."

"Good."

Thia looked into Ruff's eyes. "Dixie told me that you were special with horses. I could see that in the way that you handled this one. You've got a gentle way about you, Rufus."

He could feel Houston's eyes on him and Ruff blushed. "Most people call me Ruff."

"Now and then—when the mood strikes me—I'd like to call you Rufus."

Ruff managed a nod of his head. Feeling very uncomfortable, he stammered, "Maybe if you could go get those blankets?"

"Sure."

"I'll go with you," Dixie said.

When they were alone, Houston squatted down on his heels and ran his hand across the mare's rough coat. "All right," he drawled, "what do you really think her chances are?"

"Not good," Ruff said.

Houston digested this in silence. "If she's going to die anyway, why put Mrs. Eldee's life and farm in jeopardy? I say we put the mare out of her misery. It'd be the Christian thing to do, Ruff."

But Ruff shook his head. "We'll wait a day or two. If she stays down, we'll do what you say. But let's give the old girl a little time."

"Mrs. Eldee says that the Union patrols come by and visit pretty often. Time is one thing we are a little short of these days."

"One day," Ruff said, his voice flat and uncompromising. "This mare has probably given us ten or twelve fine colts. Let's give her a day, Houston."

He stood up, rubbed the stubble of his jaw, and nodded. "Good enough. But we'd better keep a sharp guard posted at all times. The weather is clearing and that means the road will get busy."

Ruff turned his mind off of the threat of danger. He leaned close to the mare and began to talk to her. She pricked her ears a little, which was the best she could do, and the sight and sound of the poor old gal made Ruff's heart ache.

FOUR

That night, another storm passed through and a blanket of fresh snow covered the farmyard. They had all taken turns sitting up with the old mare and, by the first light of day, it was clear that she was dying.

Ruff, Dixie, and Houston held a somber conference.

"There's no sense in prolonging her suffering," Houston said, his expression grim as he went over and pulled his Spencer rifle from its scarred leather scabbard.

"No," Ruff conceded, watching the mare as she struggled to breathe. She was so weak now that she could not have raised her head even if they had more medicine.

"Sometimes they'll come back," Dixie argued without conviction. "You've seen Father—"

"We're not our father," Ruff said, "and this isn't Wildwood Farm. We don't have the time or the medicine and maybe not the knowledge that Father had to work with."

Ruff lowered his voice. "Dixie, the mare suffers. You know that if Father was here he'd already have shot her."

Tears welled up in Dixie's eyes and Thia looked away. Houston's voice was gentle as he checked his rifle and said, "Why don't you get a harness, a singletree, and chain. We'll hitch up a span of mules to pull High Ma'am out into the woods."

"The scavengers will eat her!"

"She won't mind," Thia said, comforting Dixie. "Her spirit is already leaving her body."

"Let's go," Ruff said, taking Dixie's arm and leading her out of the barn after grabbing a couple of halters to bring in the pulling mules.

They had not gone twenty feet when Ruff heard the Spencer rifle's muffled blast from inside the barn. Dixie seemed to break in the middle. She covered her face and began to cry.

"I'll take her into the house," Thia said.

Ruff kicked at the fresh snow. He looked up at the leaden sky and felt the sting of an arctic wind. "Thanks. I'll get the mules. There's a taste of fresh snow in the air. It'll cover the drag track."

Ruff crunched through the snow. He saw a wagon pass on the road and the driver stared at him, but Ruff ignored the man. He had trouble catching the mules who kept trotting off. They cavorted, kicked, and bucked, feeling good and frisky. Ruff cussed inwardly and kept after them. He could and perhaps should have gone and saddled his own horse but he did not want to be any more visible than was necessary. Besides, his own stubbornness was as thick and unwavering as that of the mules, and Ruff was determined to wear them down until they tired of their game.

The "game" lasted almost an hour and would have lasted even longer without Houston's help. By the time they caught the big, spunky mules, then got them hitched up to a singletree, it was fully midmorning and the wind was pushing snowflakes around in the sky.

"These damned mules!" Houston puffed. "They may be smarter than horses, but they're also pains in the ass at times."

"Make that *most* of the time," Ruff corrected.

They drove the hitched mules into the barn. At the sight of the dead Thoroughbred, the mules tried to whirl and race back outside. For a few minutes, it was all that Houston and Ruff could do to control the big mules. When they finally got them under control and backed into position, Ruff chained up the hind legs of the dead Ballou mare and signaled to Houston that all was ready.

The mules knew how to play games but they also knew how to pull. They skidded the dead mare across the barn and through the door as if she were a big sheath of tobacco leaves. The mules stamped across the farmyard and were moving so fast that Houston had a tough time turning them back toward the forest.

"Keep them moving," Ruff called.

"Moving, hell! It's all I can do to keep them from running me down!"

The mules must not have gotten much use anymore because they were spunky and driving like fury. The dead mare's weight cleared snow down to the earth, leaving a broad swath of wet earth to mark their passing.

The trees were only about fifty yards behind the barn but Ruff wanted to drag the mare a long ways back into the forest. She'd freeze in the night but that wouldn't stop the coyotes and other feral animals from picking her bones.

Driving the excited mules through the heavy forest took luck and skill. The mules skidded poor High Ma'am through brush, in and out of creek beds, and banged her into trees until their progress was finally blocked by the heavy undergrowth.

"This ought to be far enough," Houston called. "Unhitch the mare and let's get back to the farm."

Ruff's fingers were numb with cold and the chain was unforgiving. He pinched a blue blister on his left thumb and finally got the chains and singletree unhooked. Cussing and shouting, he and Houston turned the mules around and jumped on their backs.

"Yaah!" Ruff shouted to the surprised mule as he slammed his heels into its ribs.

The mule tried to twist its shaggy head around and bite him on the leg. Ruff kicked it in the muzzle and then pounded its ribs again. His mule brayed and bolted for the barnyard like a racehorse off the starting line. It was all that Ruff could do to stay on the mule, what with forest branches raking him and the mule jumping deadfall, skidding through the trees, and trying to buck all at the same time.

Somehow he stayed on the mule and so did Houston. When they finally shot out of the trees, they were running almost ear to ear. When they rounded the barn and came barreling into the yard, they were whooping, laughing, and riding as if it were a high-stakes Tennessee horse race. The streaming wind made Ruff's eyes water, and it numbed his face but he figured the fun was worth the physical discomfort. Neither he nor Houston had laughed so hard in a long, long time. Ruff caught a watery glimpse of Dixie, Thia, and Margaret as they shot across the farmyard and continued into the pasture.

"Whoa!" Houston yelled. "We won!"

"The hell you did!" Ruff shouted. "*We* won!"

The point was moot because the mules were carrying them farther and farther from the barn and they didn't stop until they had run almost a quarter of a mile and skidded up against a fence so abruptly that both Houston and Ruff were launched over their heads and the fence. They somersaulted into the next pasture, hitting the snow and skidding to a stop, still laughing.

The mules raced off, braying with victory and defiance. Ruff and Houston knocked the snow from their clothes.

"You all right?" Houston asked, looking to his brother.

Ruff ran his hands over his legs, shoulders, and arms. "Sure," he said. "Easiest spill I ever took."

"Me too," Houston said, chuckling as he walked around in circles, inspecting himself and finding no injuries.

They climbed back through the fence, watching the mules buck and run, but then the gangly beasts suddenly stopped and pricked their ears toward the road.

Ruff and Houston instinctively followed the line of the mules' ears and their hearts nearly froze when they saw about ten riders trotting briskly up the lane. It wasn't an army patrol but it wasn't a social visit, either. The men were all heavily armed and they looked grim and determined. Ruff knew at a glance they were deserters or a group of scavengers, the likes of which were commonplace through the devastated South. There was no law left other than the law of the gun.

"Oh, sweet Jesus!" Houston cried, his hand stabbing for the gun on his hip but coming up empty.

Ruff was unarmed as well. He watched helplessly as the riders split in half and drew their weapons, half going on into the farmyard, half coming toward them.

"We'll try and bluff this thing out," Houston said, moving close and speaking in a low, measured tone.

"What are you going to tell them?"

"I have no idea. Mainly, I'm just going to try and keep us alive until we can get our weapons."

Ruff nodded. He was furious at himself for not strapping on his Colt, although it probably would not have made much difference against so many. Their only hope, as Houston suggested, was to try and talk their way through the trouble. These were very hard-looking men, the dregs of war who would kill without thought or remorse.

"Morning!" Houston called, raising his right hand in greeting and forcing a strained smile.

Ruff smiled, too. His eyes flicked to the farmhouse, where the other five men were dismounting. He thought he saw Margaret on the porch, a rifle in her hands, but he could not be sure. All he was sure of was that they were in a real bad fix. It would not be all that surprising if the five men now approaching them simply shot them and rode back to the farmhouse and had their way with the women.

The leader was unremarkable except that he was missing his left arm. Missing limbs were commonplace these days and they hardly attracted any attention. He wore a wild black beard and his eyes were hooded by a low, heavy brow. Like those at his side, he wore parts of Confederate and Union army uniforms. And like his companions, he carried a carbine clenched in his dirty hands.

The five riders pulled their horses up short. For several moments, they just studied Houston and Ruff with hard, calculating eyes.

"Afternoon," Houston said again, his smile brittle as brass. "Pretty good storm we had last night, huh?"

The leader's eyes carried out to the fence, then followed the swath of earth that marked where the dead Thoroughbred had been dragged. Ruff could not even begin to guess what was on the one-armed man's mind.

"Dead horse?" he finally asked, not looking at either of them but instead, between them.

"Yeah," Houston said. "Died last night."

When the one-armed man did not offer a comment, Ruff said, "But she was an old mare."

"You boys live here?"

Ruff glanced at Houston who said, "We're just passing through this country. These people are kinfolks."

The one-armed man twisted around in his McClelland saddle, spitting a stream of brown tobacco juice into the bright, white snow. He watched as the five men who had gone to farmhouse dismounted with their rifles held up before their chests.

"You married to either of them wimmen?" he asked as the distant sound of angry words carried across the pasture.

"No." Houston took a step closer to the one-armed man's horse but was brought up short when one of the riders raised and cocked his carbine.

Ruff stuffed his hands into his coat, desperate to find something to grab and hurl if it became obvious they were going to be shot.

"Git yore goddamn hands out where I kin see 'em," a man hissed.

Ruff pulled out his hands and raised them a little. He was about to say something when there was a gunshot from the farmhouse. He heard a woman scream and involuntarily rocked forward.

"Freeze!"

Ruff froze. His eyes whipped from the one-armed man to the farmhouse, which the five riders had stormed. There were two more shots. Ruff felt his heart hammer violently against his chest. His hands clenched into fists. He glanced at Houston, and his brother was as white as the snow at their feet.

"What are you going to do?" Houston managed to ask.

"You boys got any money or anything of value on your persons?"

"Got some money," Houston said, "but not much."

Two more shots banked across the snow-covered pasture. The one-armed man said, "Jess, you, Abe, and Nate gallop over to the house and tell the boys I don't want 'em to hurt any ladies, hear now?"

The three men wheeled their horses and galloped away, hooves cupping and hurling balls of ice and snow.

"You got anything of value?" the leader said, jerking his carbine in Ruff's direction.

Ruff's mind spun like a coin. His first impulse was to say no, but something told him that would be a fatal mistake.

"I got a little money and a watch and chain. It belonged to my father."

"Now it's gonna belong to me," the one-armed man said with a cruel smile. "Let's see it."

Ruff reached for the top button of his coat and as he did, his hand whipped up, snatched his hat from his head, and he swatted the one-armed man's horse across the eyes.

The animal whirled away in fright and Ruff threw himself at the one-armed man. He heard the carbine bark but didn't feel a thing as his big hands clamped on the man's arm and yanked him from his saddle.

Another rifle shot caused Ruff to stagger but he didn't let go of his man as he dragged him to the ground. Ruff heard Houston grunt as he drew back his boot and drove it into the side of the one-armed man's head. Stunned, the man's mouth flew open, black teeth and rotting gums framed by his black beard. Ruff kicked the man again in the ear and he quivered, making low, choking sounds.

Another shot caused Ruff to pivot around in time to see Houston climb off the other killer, who rolled over onto his stomach and began to try and drag himself toward the farmhouse.

Anyone but a horseman would have rushed the two rider-less horses and probably have scared them into a run, but not Houston or Ruff. They both slowed their motion and began to talk to the horses.

"You're bleeding from the shoulder," Houston said, never taking his eyes off the horse he stalked.

"It can't be much," Ruff replied, his voice calm and sooth-ing as he kept his eyes on the snorting horse as it backed

away, eyes rolling in fear, nostrils twitching at the scent of
fresh blood.

"Easy, easy," Ruff chanted, mixing in a few Cherokee
words as he advanced, eyes on the horse and the trailing
reins that now dragged enticingly across the snow.

The horse was going to whirl and race back to the others
at the farm. Ruff was sure of it, so he dived for the reins.
Caught them and held on as the terrified animal whirled and
tried to run. Ruff would not let loose. The horse dragged him
several yards and then, with its head twisted back around, it
was forced to stop. A moment later, Ruff had the animal
under control. He turned just in time to accept the carbine
that Houston held out to him.

"What now?" Ruff asked, turning toward the farmhouse.
If their count was right, there were eight more riders inside
the house doing God only knew what to Dixie, Thia, and
Margaret.

"We can't stand up against 'em with just these two single-
shot rifles," Houston said, jamming boot into stirrup and
mounting the horse. "Let's get armed."

Ruff shifted the one-armed man's carbine into his right
hand and used his left to grab the mane and vault onto
the horse, reining and kicking it into a run. He knew as
well as Houston that if they were seen, they'd be shot out
of their saddles before they could reach the barn, where
their own weapons, along with their Thoroughbreds, were
waiting.

They made it to the barn, but only because either Dixie
or Thia was raising hell inside the house. Ruff could hear
the pair screaming, and his blood froze as he jumped from
his horse and grabbed his Army Colt, strapping it on. He had
two more Colts that he'd confiscated from the battlefield, and
when Houston had his Spencer repeating rifle in his hands,
they both charged out of the barn.

"I'll go in the front door, you circle around to the back,"
Ruff said.

A flash of protest welled in Houston's eyes but Ruff was
already moving past him, six-guns in both hands. He was

the better man with a pistol and what awaited them inside
the farmhouse was going to be close, fast, and bloody pistol work.

Ruff lost his footing on the front porch steps and crashed
down hard, but he jumped back to his feet, grabbed the door,
and tore it open to see a knot of men surrounding Thia and
Dixie, who were down and kicking.

Ruff didn't bother to lift his gun and aim. The Army
Colts in his fists bucked fire, lead, and smoke. Everything
happened so fast that he did not see things distinctly. It was
a collage of images. Of men twisting around to face him with
wild eyes transforming lust to terror.

Dirty, ragged men clawing for guns. Mouths flying open,
vacant and stretched with screams. Smoke and thunder. Flying bodies. Now the sounds of Houston's Spencer rifle boom-
ing in the hallway.

More screaming. Falling. Hitting a couch and still pulling
the trigger. The sound of a battlefield locked and amplified
within walls. Splashes of red and orange. The ominous click
of empty guns, and then moans and gasps and the sound of
Thia's swirling black hair shrouding Ruff's face, spiraling
him into a silent abyss.

It was dark when Ruff awoke and opened his eyes to
see Dixie and Thia at his bedside. He tried to sit up but
a burning needle pierced his skull and brought a groan to
his lips.

"Don't move," Thia said, placing her hand on his shoulder.
"You've been shot but it's not too serious."

"Again?" Ruff closed his eyes. He shifted a little and
now the pain in his shoulder made him flinch. "What about
Houston?"

"He did a little better."

Ruff opened his eyes. "And the others?"

Thia looked away quickly. Ruff saw a nasty bruise on her
cheek. The memory of her and Dixie on the floor, kicking
and screaming as they fought to keep the men from them hit
him hard.

"Dixie? Are you all right?"

"Yes," she said, taking his hand in her own. "I killed one of them, Ruff. I shot him coming through the door. Thia shot one, too."

"I only wounded him," Thia whispered. "Houston finished him in the hallway."

Ruff expelled a deep, ragged breath. "They're all dead?"

Dixie squeezed his hand even tighter. "So is Mrs. Eldee. She had an old shotgun all ready. Hit the first one through the door full in the chest but the second one shot her."

Dixie's voice shook. "Oh, Ruff, I was sure that you and Houston were shot to death out there in the pasture. And when you came rushing into the house, firing both those guns, I . . ."

Ruff lifted his hand and he placed his fingers on her lips. "It's over, Dixie. And as soon as we can, we're leaving the South, forever. There is no turning back for us. There's been too much bloodshed. Too much death."

A tear cascaded down Dixie's cheek. "I know," she managed to say. "Thia has been telling me all about the Indian Territory. It sounds beautiful, Ruff. It sounds like someplace where we can start over again."

Ruff looked at Thia. He could see that her eyes were red and swollen. That told him that Thia had cared for Mrs. Eldee a lot more than she'd shown on the surface.

"We've got to leave right away," Ruff said. "I can feel the danger and it's just a matter of time before someone else comes along."

"We can hitch the mules to the wagon and load up what we have to," she said. "You're not fit to ride yet."

"What's Houston doing?"

"He's digging . . ." Thia struggled with the painful words. " . . . digging Margaret's grave. He's got a lantern. There's a little cemetery out back behind the house."

Ruff understood. "What about your grandfolks?"

"Granddad doesn't understand. Grandma won't leave."

"She *has* to leave!" Ruff said. "It's not safe here. They're not fit to stay by themselves."

"Grandma is stubborn," Thia said. "We've still got some Negroes who want to stay and help. It's what she wants to do."

"But . . ."

"They're *old*," Thia said. "They'd die on the way to the Indian Territory. They want to be buried here. Beside their children."

Ruff could see that it was pointless to argue further. "All right," he said, reaching out, his fingertips just brushing Thia's bruised cheek. "But you're coming?"

Her dark eyes were rimmed red and wet with tears but her voice left no doubt of her strong conviction. "Yes!"

Ruff managed a smile. He shifted his gaze to Dixie. "Tell Houston I want to leave in the morning as soon as we've laid Mrs. Eldee to rest."

"It's what he wants to do, too," Dixie said.

Ruff sighed and tried to think clearly. "I guess we can take all the livestock, the ten horses . . . what are we going to do, bury all of those murderers?"

Dixie swallowed. "Me and Houston took their bodies out in the forest. Near High Ma'am."

Ruff dipped his chin with understanding. In this freezing winter weather, just digging one grave for Mrs. Eldee was going to be a backbreaking job, ten more graves would have been impossible.

"How far," Ruff asked, "is it to the Indian Territory?"

Thia considered the question for a moment, then said, "A little more than a hundred miles."

"Four or five days and we'll be there," Ruff said, trying to sound hopeful. "Then this war will be behind us and we can think about building a new life again."

Thia started to say something but closed her mouth and nodded in grave silence. Ruff got lost in the dark, liquid pools of her eyes, and he swam in her beauty and her sorrow until he drifted off to sleep again and dreamed of a clean, unspoiled land that had yet to hear the sound of cannon or to taste the corruption of war.

FIVE

If anything, the weather had deteriorated by the next morning. The winds had shifted just before dawn and were now gusting from the west. Tree branches whipped the dark sky and the temperature did not climb above freezing all morning.

Ruff stared out of the window, his mood as dark and miserable as the weather. He could see Houston and one of the Negroes lower Margaret into a grave that Houston had chopped through the frost line. Thia, Dixie, and the frail old Mrs. Eldee stood huddled beside the grave, draped in heavy black shawls. Dirty-bottomed storm clouds lurched around overhead, stabbing occasional bolts of lightning at the earth. Somewhere in another part of the house, Ruff could hear the simple-minded Mr. Eldee holding an animated, nonsensical conversation with himself in two distinctly childish voices.

Ruff watched as they lowered Margaret Eldee into the grave beside that of her late husband. He wondered if there was anyone in the South whose life had not been touched and marred if not outright destroyed by the Civil War. Ruff tried to imagine what Margaret had been like before the war. Had she been pleasant and happy with empathy and kindness and love toward her fellow man? Had she and her husband been in love and walked hand in hand down their gravel lane, smelling the spring flowers or feeling the warmth of a summer breeze on their faces? Had they shared a vision for themselves and believed—as most of Southerners had once believed—that the good life in Dixie would last forever?

Ruff watched his brother and the Negro bow their heads along with the women. The prayer was very brief, and then Houston took a shovel up and the Negro helped him fill the grave.

"Things will get better for us," Ruff pledged aloud. "This war can't last forever and things will get better."

But even as he said this, Ruff doubted his own words. The South might heal physically, but he knew that it would fester in defeat for generations. There was so much pride and pain that this war would not be forgotten in a hundred years. In just four years, a way of life had been shattered and then trampled in the dirt.

Ruff sat up, clenched his teeth from the pain in his head, and began to dress. He felt dizzy and weak but was sure that both these afflictions would pass in a few days, a week at the most. By then, they'd be in the Indian Territory. They'd claim land, use what money and things of value they possessed to start over again. Maybe they would have to do things other than raising horses in order to get by, but Ruff knew that neither he nor his brother or even Dixie were above hard work.

Two hours later, the mules were hitched, the wagon was loaded, and all the good-byes had been said. Ruff was riding in the wagon while Houston drove. Dixie rode High Man and his son, High Fire, was tethered to the wagon on the opposite side of their mares. Both stallions were animated again because of the rest, grain, and cold weather. Their three mares and the horses they'd collected from the dead mauraders were quiet and resigned to travel.

Thia was the last to mount a horse and she stood talking low to her grandmother and grandfather for several minutes. Ruff could see that she was almost in tears, and the old lady actually was crying. Grandfather Eldee, being simple, was spared the pain of this sad parting.

When Thia did turn her back on the old couple and mount her horse, Ruff heard a low, involuntary sob tear from her throat. He wished that he was as good with words as Houston so that he could say something wise and comforting, but no words came to him. It seemed that everyone was saying good-byes these days, sometimes over a cold grave, sometimes to folks they loved and never expected to see again. Ruff nodded his head to let Thia know he understood. He gripped his brother's Spencer repeating rifle and hoped that he would not have to use it on their road to the Indian Territory.

Thia quickly proved that she knew this country like the back of her own hand. She selected a little-used farm road that was deeply rutted. The snow turned to slush by noon and the going was slow and sloppy.

That first night, they found shelter at an abandoned farm. It was obvious that the place had been looted and sacked. The windows were all busted out and the floor was covered with broken glass. There had once been a cornfield but it had been burned and used to feed hobbled livestock. A flower and vegetable garden had been trampled almost beyond recognition.

There was little to be cheerful about that evening for the wind blew cold through the open windows and melted snow had left some six-foot oblong depressions in the front yard that were undoubtedly shallow graves. The whole place gave them a sad, eerie feeling, and Ruff heard Thia arise long before dawn and then go out to the barn to check the horses.

He had not slept well himself and went out to join her. Feeling much stronger after a day of rest, Ruff was sure that he would be fine on horseback the remainder of the journey.

Thia was standing in the barn and had just turned up the wick on the lamp when Ruff stepped inside.

"Tough night?" he asked after a moment as he watched the Cherokee girl walk over and stroke the soft muzzle of one of the Ballou mares.

Thia turned quickly but when she saw Ruff standing beside the barn door, she relaxed. "I felt as if that farmhouse was haunted with ghosts. I felt very uneasy inside its walls. Didn't you?"

"Kind of," Ruff admitted. "But with the weather so cold, there wasn't much choice. At least we could get the stove cracking and popping and didn't have to freeze."

Thia reached into her coat pocket and walked over to Ruff. "Look," she said, unable to contain her excitement as she held out a small locket and chain. The locket was obviously solid gold, shiny, exquisite, and etched with filagree. Ruff had seen many such lockets worn by debutantes in the South, and this would have been prized by any of them.

Thia's left forefinger traced the etching and caressed the beautiful locket. "Ruff, I found this in the yard. It was almost completely buried in the dirt. But just the smallest length of chain caught the sun and then my eye. I couldn't believe my eyes when I pulled it out of the mud and slush."

Ruff held the locket in the palm of his open hand and admired the workmanship and its tiny hinge. "Thia, did you open it?"

"No."

"Why not?"

"I feel as if it would be wrong. The locket isn't mine. It belongs to someone and there might be something personal inside. A picture or some special words of affection. It . . . it would be almost like evesdropping. Or opening someone's letter that you found."

"But it might give you a clue as to its real owner."

"Maybe. But I doubt it."

Ruff handed the locket back to the Cherokee girl. Thia stared at it for so long that Ruff shifted his feet and said, "What are you going to do with it?"

"I'm not sure. Any ideas?"

"Wear it. If the owner recognizes it, give it back. Otherwise, what good is a locket that is hidden in a box? You can't enjoy it and there would be no chance it would ever be found."

"Yes," Thia said with smile, "I was thinking the very same thing, but then I told myself I was just trying to come up with a selfish reason to wear it."

"No you weren't." Ruff took the locket from her hands. He fumbled with the chain's tiny clasp until she unlatched it for him, and then she lifted her long, black hair and turned away.

When Ruff raised the locket to her lovely neck, his hands shook. Feeling stupid, he took a deep breath, but when he touched Thia's hair and the soft skin on her neck, his hands shook even harder.

"Ruff, what's taking you so long?" she asked. "Have you changed your mind and decided I shouldn't wear it after all?"

"Oh no!" he said in much too loud a voice as he clumsily draped the chain and locket around her neck and then struggled with the clasp.

He expelled an audible sigh of relief when he got the damned thing locked. She turned and her eyes looking right up into his made Ruff's knees knock. He gulped.

"How do you like it?" she whispered.

"What?"

Her lips lifted at the corners and she leaned back a little and then thrust her chest out at him. "The locket?"

"Oh yes!" His eyes dropped to the soft, hollow place at the base of her throat and his mouth went so dry he had to work up spittle just to unstick his tongue from the roof of his mouth. "The locket!"

"Do you like it?" she repeated, rising up on her toes and closing her eyes.

"It's beautiful," he breathed, kissing her mouth.

Thia melted into his arms like warm syrup. She seemed to mold to his body and Ruff's poor head began pounding so fiercely that he became dizzy and had to break away lest he humiliate himself and fall dumbstruck to the barn's floor.

Thia stepped back a little and she looked as cool as the frost on pumpkins. She was watching him very closely, a slightly amused look on her pretty face.

"Ruff, is something wrong?"

"No," he managed to reply.

"Do you want to kiss me again?"

He did and he did. The second time was better, and this time it was Thia who had to end their embrace and looked as rattled as he felt.

"Well," she said a little breathlessly, "what do you think?"

"I still think you ought to wear the locket," he blurted.

She giggled. "That's not what I meant."

"What did you mean?"

"Are we going to get married?"

"Huh!"

She blinked and her smile slipped a little. "When a Cherokee man kisses a Cherokee girl, I was always taught that it meant the man wanted to marry the girl."

"Now wait a minute," Ruff said, pressing his forefingers to his temples, and retreating a step. "I never heard such a thing before."

"That's because you don't know very much about the Cherokee yet. But don't worry. When we reach the Indian Territory and join those that have not forsaken their culture, you'll learn plenty."

Ruff nodded vigorously. "Well, Thia, that might well be, but it don't change the fact that I don't consider a kiss the equal of proposal of marriage."

Her lips turned downward. "Well just what—if anything— does it mean to you?"

"It means you make my knees knock and my heart slam," he said without thinking. "It means that I think you're beautiful and brave. It means I like to be around you, even at dawn in this cold old barn with ghosts swirling around through the cobwebs and the rafters."

The anger in Thia's eyes faded. "That's pretty nice," she said. "In fact, it's real nice. And I guess you've kissed a few girls before, haven't you?"

He nodded. "A few."

"Quite a few, I'll bet."

"Some. But none as pretty as you."

She leaned against his chest. "That's a sweet thing to say, Ruff. I like you and even with your missing earlobe I still think you're handsome."

"Really?"

"Sure!"

"Houston is the handsome one of us," Ruff said, shamelessly angling for further reassurances.

"Well, he *is* very handsome," Thia admitted, "but he knows it. You don't. And besides, he told me he was still in love with that spy he met named Molly O'Day."

"Yeah," Ruff said. "He forgets most girls the next morning, or at least after a few days. But not Molly. He swears that he's going to go find her after getting us settled in Oklahoma."

"He'll get himself killed if he goes to the North. We should try and talk him into staying with the Cherokee."

"Oh, Dixie and I will," Ruff pledged. "But Houston has always been the kind that, the harder you try to push him one way, the harder he pushes back. Pa used to say that about all of us. Dixie isn't much better."

"She said the same thing about you," Thia said with a smile.

Ruff laughed. He reached out and touched the locket and then he took Thia's hand and they grained and watered the horses.

An hour later, they were on the road again and the storm clouds were breaking into blue sky.

Ruff was in love. Despite everyone's protests, he'd insisted on riding High Fire, and he made no pretense about riding next to anyone but Thia. They rode out ahead of the wagon, feeling the sun on their faces and stealing frequent sideways glances at each other.

Sometimes that day when they passed a cemetery or other abandoned or destroyed farms, Ruff felt a heavy sense of guilt over his happiness. It seemed terribly unfair that he should have found such a beautiful girl that thought him handsome while Houston was pining over Molly O'Day and everyone else in the South was mourning the losses of loved ones dead or missing in battle.

But as the miles passed, Ruff's sense of guilt faded as he came to decide that for a long time he had mourned the death of his brothers, mother, and father. Their absence had left a deep, empty place in his heart that would never completely be filled. Not by Thia or anyone else. And if nothing else, the war had taught him that there were no guarantees in life.

That a person just needed to live more for the present and to squeeze as much joy and happiness as he could from every single day.

That evening, they came to a farming town in eastern Arkansas called Maple Forks. It was sundown and they were all exhausted and the weather was clear but very cold.

"Let's see if we can find us some rooms at the hotel and a livery big enough to put all our horses and these mules up for the night," Houston suggested.

"Do you think that's the wisest thing to do?" Ruff asked. "Could be this town is in Union hands."

"It probably is," Houston said, standing up in the wagon and shading his eyes. "But my guess is that it's like most in that we'll not be bothered if we keep to ourselves."

Ruff looked to Dixie and Thia, and their expressions told him that they were dead tired and anxious for a real feather bed, a warm fire, and food.

"All right. But I'd better ride in first just to make sure that there are no soldiers."

But Houston had his own ideas. He cracked the lines across the rumps of the mules and drove the wagon on toward town. "We're almost in Oklahoma," he said. "If the war isn't over yet, it's far, far to the east of us."

"I hope he's right," Dixie said with a look of real concern.

"Me too," Ruff said as he joined Thia and Dixie and hurried after his brother.

Maple Fork looked untouched by war. They saw no Union patrols or uniforms, and the town was as peaceful as a church social. They found a livery where a man was more than willing to board all their horses and the mules for a fair price.

"You'll find that the Howard house just up the street is the best place for the ladies. You men will want to stay at Maple Inn."

"This looks like a fine town," Ruff said, shouldering his saddlebags, canteen, and extra Army Colts.

"Oh, we have our share of hell raising," the liveryman said. "Just down at the end of town is a gamblin' place called Diamond Jake's Palace. They got pretty wimmen, good whiskey, and plenty of card games for a man to squander his hard-earned money on."

Houston perked right up at this bit of news. "Honest games?"

"Hell no!" the liveryman scoffed. "But the wimmen are pretty and the liquor is the best I ever drank."

The edge of a grin tugged up the corners of Houston's mouth. "Maybe, Ruff, we ought to stop by and have ourselves a couple of drinks."

"Not me," Ruff said. "I think we'd just better stay to our rooms and rest."

"Aw," Houston scoffed, "We're long overdue for a little fun! A few drinks sure won't hurt us any and it might well do us some good."

"In that case," the liveryman said, "you'd better pay me and the hotels in advance. Diamond Jake ain't known as a man who lets money walk out of his place of business."

"Is that right," Houston said, his eyes sparkling with amusement, "well, I'll just have to see if I can't change that reputation a mite before we leave this town."

"A lot have tried and damn few have succeeded, mister."

Dixie caught Ruff's eye and he could see the worry in her expression. But what could he do once Houston decided that he was overdue to have a little fun and excitement? If you told Houston he couldn't do a thing it just made him all the more determined to do it.

"Maybe I'll come along and have a drink after all to keep you company," Ruff heard himself say.

"Suit yourself," Houston said with indifference. "But just don't try to nursemaid or drag me out of there until I'm ready to go."

Ruff nodded. They hadn't been in Maple Fork an hour and he was already sorry they hadn't camped out this cold night in the woods. The Indian Territory was still another fifty miles away and before they reached it, a lot more could go wrong than right.

SIX

Diamond Jack's Palace wasn't anything more than a big barn converted into a saloon, dance hall, and gambling den. True, it was a cut above most saloons in that it had some big "girlie" pictures with gilded frames, a mahogany bar some seventy feet long, and one immense chandelier whose hanging crystals had mostly been shot off.

The dice, faro, and gambling tables were worn of their green felt tops and the floor was covered with the usual sawdust, although it did look to be cleaner than most found in a barnyard. When Ruff and Houston entered Diamond Jack's, there was a crowd of about seventy men of every description. A woman in black tights was dancing and singing on a big table but she was so fat and listless that nobody paid her the slightest bit of attention.

"Didn't that liveryman say something about pretty women working here?" Houston asked cryptically as they edged their way toward the bar.

"He did," Ruff said, watching and listening carefully to the men all around. He quickly determined that this was an all-Southern clientele, and most of the patrons were actually wearing articles of Confederate uniforms.

Ruff relaxed. "I hope he wasn't also lying about the quality of the whiskey."

"We'll soon find out," Houston said, squeezing his way in between a couple of men to wedge himself up against the bar.

The two men he'd separated gave Houston a hard look, and one was about to say something when, out of the corner of

56

his eye, he spotted Ruff and decided to swallow his objection. The noise was so loud that Ruff didn't realize until it arrived that Houston had ordered a bottle rather than just a couple of shots.

Houston filled two dirty glasses to the brim and twisted around to hand Ruff his glass. "To new beginnings," he said, raising his glass in toast. "And to Dixie!"

Ruff nodded, toasted, and drank. Swallowing the whiskey was like a swallowing a burning ember. He gasped and choked as whiskey flowing like lava scorched its way down to his belly, where it seemed to give off smoke and sparks. Ruff squeezed his eyes shut and tears ran down his tanned cheeks. He opened his eyes and scrubbed them dry with the back of his hand.

"Kee—rist!" he wheezed. "This whiskey is terrible!"

Houston barked a hoarse laugh. He looked down at his empty glass, then poured himself another another. "Ruff, good times are damned few and far between these days. A man has to take what precious pleasures he can, where he can."

Ruff cleared his seared throat. "Let's get out of here. Bring that bottled lightning if you want, but there's nothing here for us."

"There's nothing for us back in that hotel room, either," Houston said, tossing down more whiskey. "But if that suits your style, then you go on back and get your rest. What I need is some good times and laughter."

Ruff shook his head. He could see by the determined set of Houston's square jaw that the man wasn't going to budge from the bar for a while. Later, he'd find himself a place at one of the card games and settle in for the night. If Houston was lucky and stayed reasonably sober, maybe he'd win a little money. But if Houston got drunk, the way he appeared determined to do, then things were going to go downhill fast. Ruff had seen his brother in this kind of "to-hell-with-everything" attitude before and it always spelled trouble.

"We got a long day of travel tomorrow," Ruff said, "besides, we've got some talking to do in private."

"The hell we do," Houston said, his eyes taking on a shine as he watched the fat woman dance and sing before he turned his attention to the gambling tables, where greenback dollars as well as gold and silver coin were changing hands. There wasn't any Confederate money being bet in this Arkansas thieve's den, and that spoke more than words the tragic state of the war and the Confederacy.

Ruff knew that he had to either leave his brother and return to a soft, warm bed where he could get some badly needed sleep, or remain here with his only living brother and try to keep Houston out of trouble.

Houston drank deeply. "What do we have to talk about in private?"

"Just things," Ruff said. "We have to make some decisions before we reach the Indian Territory."

"Such as?" Houston challenged.

"Such as whether or not we plan to stay and build, or wait until the war is over and go back to Wildwood Farm and rebuild what must have been destroyed by General Sherman as he marched through on his way to Atlanta."

Houston snickered. "Hell, we *can't* go back! Haven't you even figured that much out yet?"

Stung by his brother's rebuke, Ruff bristled. "We can go back if we want. It's been our home, our land for as long as we've been alive. And our parents and brothers are buried there! What do you mean, we can't go back!"

"Maybe you've forgotten about Captain Denton and Lieutenant Pike?"

Ruff stiffened. "I don't think this is the place to talk about them," he said, looking from side to side at the hard faces of strangers.

"Why not?" Houston demanded, his manner reckless and aggressive. "They tried to take the last of our horses. The captain let our brother die in battle while he escaped on one of our mares. That's why we shot him and later that murdering lieutenant and his men."

The conversation along their end of the bar died.

"Let's get on back to the hotel and call it a night," Ruff said, grabbing his brother's arm.

But Houston shook it off. "I'm not ready to go yet," he said. "But you asked about Tennessee and I told you how it is with us now, Ruff. We can't ever go back."

Ruff wanted to drive his fist into the point of Houston's handsome jaw and drop him like a stone, but even more, he wanted to keep peace in what was left of the family and drag Houston out of this saloon and gambling hall before they both got into big trouble.

"So we'll build a new horse farm in the Indian Territory," Ruff said. "We'll start over and—"

"Uh-uh," Houston said. "We'll go there and maybe even stay a month or two, but only long enough to win a few horse races and pick up some traveling money."

This was news to Ruff. "I thought we were going to settle and rebuild."

"No," Houston said. "We're going to do some traveling and horse racing. I got my heart set on Texas but not until I've gone to Washington, D.C., and found Molly O'Day."

Ruff thought of his sister. Thought of how Dixie had done little else except talk about her mother's Cherokee people and how she wanted to learn more about them. And he thought about Thia and how she shared the same dream of returning to the Cherokees and building something in Oklahoma.

And finally, Ruff suddenly realized that he was also looking forward to settling down in the Indian Territory. Maybe not forever. He still toyed with the perhaps unrealistic hope that he and what remained of the Ballous might someday return to Tennessee. The Great Smoky Mountains were his idea of beautiful country and the Tennessee forests ran as deep as the marrow of his Rebel bones.

"Maybe Texas is wrong for us," Ruff said, knowing he sounded feeble but determined not to get into a public and angry quarrel with his brother.

"In that case, we'll keep traveling west," Houston announced. "I'm done with the South. It's finished and the ashes won't be worth picking through."

"Mister," a buckskin-clad man with a bowie knife in his belt said, "unless I overheard wrong, you boys have and killed Southern officers and now you're deserting the South in the time of its greatest need."

Houston poured himself another glass of whiskey but this time, he sipped on it and just stared at the man for about a minute before he said, "I don't believe I've been speaking to you, sir. So unless you're looking to get hurt real bad, I'd stay out of what does not concern you."

The buckskin man was taller than Houston but not as tall as Ruff. He was scarred and looked hard as nails, while Houston had a way of looking a little smaller than he actually was and, when confronted, quite disarming. And never more so than now.

Ruff's eyes flicked from the buckskin man to his many friends, all of whom appeared to be the kind who made bad enemies.

"Let's go," Ruff said, reaching for Houston. "We got a long day ahead of us tomorrow."

But Houston's bright black eyes were fixed pugnaciously on the big man and his friends. He swirled the whiskey around and around in his glass and there was a go-to-hell look on his face that bordered on cockiness.

"Maybe," the big man said, "we should all step outside?"

Houston chuckled. "Naw! My brother wanted me to do that and I declined his invitation, why shouldn't I decline yours?"

"Because," the man said, reaching for his big bone-handled knife, "I ain't just askin', I'm tellin'!"

Houston whipped the glassful of whiskey across their faces with one hand and brought the whiskey bottle crashing down on the man's forehead with the other.

The buckskin man staggered and screamed, clasping his forehead, which was covered with embedded glass splinters. Houston grabbed his ears and brought his face down on a lifting knee, and the big man struck the bar so hard he went right over the top.

Ruff's fist came up from his knee level and caught one of the men in the solar plexus the way his older brothers had taught him in a most painful lesson. The man's mouth flew open and Ruff dropped him with a chopping left to the side of the face.

For the next two or three minutes, they were in a whale of a good fight. Men swinging and cursing, grunting and spitting teeth and blood. Ruff was knocked down twice, and he stayed down a moment before grabbing someone by the knees and tossing him over the bar. Ruff heard Houston laugh, and then he heard glass shatter from behind the bar. Ruff realized that the entire saloon had become involved in the melee. He saw men swinging bottles and chairs and even trying to lift tables.

"*Now* can we get out of here!" Ruff shouted.

"Yeah!" Houston bellowed, snatching a full bottle from the bar, ducking a punch and diving for the front door.

Ruff saw the fat lady who'd been trying to sing and dance raise a chair and splinter it over the head of a man who went down as if shot between the eyes with a minnie ball. He gave a loud Rebel yell and barreled outside after Houston. They sprinted down the street and dashed into their hotel just as gunfire erupted from Diamond Jake's Palace.

The hotel clerk had been reading a newspaper, but at the sight of the bloodied Ruff and Houston, the paper fell from his hands and he gaped. "Good heavens!" he cried. "Are you going to live!"

Ruff scrubbed a forearm across his face and saw smeared blood. "We are," he said, checking the rest of himself for further damage but finding none. "Houston?"

"Let's drink in our own gentlemanly company and have that private talk!" Houston roared, waving his bottle over-head.

Ruff linked his arm through his brother's. He knew that Houston was responsible for the fight and the subsequent destruction that were still taking place at Diamond Jake's Palace. He knew, too, that it would be a good thing if they left Maple Fork sometime before daybreak to avoid serious repercussions.

But Houston's eyes sparkled with merriment and he looked happy for the first time since he had lost Molly O'Day. Houston looked like . . . well, like he used to look before the war after a night of carousing and womanizing in Chattanooga.

So despite his own personal reservations, Ruff decided that he would go up and have a few drinks with his hell-raising brother and talk of nothing serious at all. Perhaps they'd share a few good memories of home and hearth. And maybe, with a few more glasses of the awful whiskey, they'd both laugh and forget the hell of a dying South and a victorious Union.

Maybe.

SEVEN

Ruff had a slight hangover the next morning when they rolled out of Maple Fork just before first light. Houston was in much worse shape and the grayness of his face matched the belly of the clouds that threatened sleet or snow.

Thia and Dixie were in much better spirits. They talked incessantly about the Indian Territory, which they hoped to reach before nightfall. Ruff was more than content to just listen and learn from Thia, who knew the entire history of the Cherokee people.

"Their traditional lands were in Georgia, the Carolinas, and your Great Smoky Mountains in eastern Tennessee. They were a flourishing civilization and a pure one until the French fur trappers and then the British intruded on their lands and intermarried among them. That is why the current principle chief of the Cherokee is John Ross, a mixed-blood like ourselves."

Thia closed her eyes. "When you meet the full-bloods in Indian Territory, you will see that they believe in the old ways. They are traditionalists without slaves or property. They believe in living in small forest communities, where they hunt and do a little farming of corn, beans, squash, and pumpkins. Their houses are made the old ways, with grasses, leaves, and tree bark. Most live in one- or two-room log cabins but a few have built mud houses like their ancestors."

"Mud houses?" asked Ruff, who had never heard of them.

"Yes, you might see them hidden in the forest. They are supported by upright poles with reeds woven in between

63

and covered with mud. The roofs are of thatch or over-lapped bark. The men wear breechcloths in the summer, deerskins their women have tanned are worn during these colder months. In the old days they lived in villages and each village had a war chief and a peace chief. The peace chief is always a woman."

Thia looked directly into Ruff's eyes. "The woman is always the head of a Cherokee family. All her children become members of her family, not the father's."

Houston snickered. "I beg to differ with you on that, Miss Eldee. Among the Indians, a squaw is just a squaw."

Thia did not get angry but her brow knotted and she was very firm when she said, "If that's the case, I guess you've never heard of the Beloved Woman named Nancy Ward."

"Who's that?"

"She lived about a hundred years ago. When she was just sixteen, she was in a terrible battle with our enemy, the Creeks, at Tali'wa, in what is now the state of Georgia. Nancy was loading rifles for her husband and our people, who, being greatly outnumbered by the Creeks, were losing the battle. Nancy Ward's husband was shot and killed, and rather than drop his weapons and run, Nancy attacked the Creeks, not caring anymore if she lived or died. Her courage was so great that it inspired her retreating tribesmen to attack with the ferocity of the cougar. The Cherokee routed their hated Creek enemies and those people never again returned to try to steal Cherokee hunting lands. Nancy Ward was honored with the title, Beloved Woman of the Cherokee."

Thia managed to award Houston with a cold smile. "Now, Mr. Ballou, does that square with your theory that 'a squaw is just a squaw'?"

Despite his hangover, Houston managed a wry grin. "There are always exceptions, like your Nancy Ward."

"Cherokee men have always respected their women," Thia said, glancing at Ruff. "Nancy Ward and other Beloved Women of the Cherokee before her have always been the voice of wisdom and reason for our people."

"It's different among the whites," Houston said, sounding a little miffed.

"That may be so," Thia argued, "but even though you are only part Cherokee, you must feel the pull of the Cherokee ways."

"I don't feel no such thing!" Houston blurted. "Thia, you're a fine girl but I think you've got a lot of crazy ideas. Being the oldest, I know a little more than Ruff or Dixie about the Indians, and there's room for improvement."

"How? Who has broken every treaty between the Cherokee and the American government? The whites! Over and over again the Cherokee have believed the United States and taken its word of honor to abide by the treaties it signs. Over and over the Cherokee have given up their lands for promises. First they were driven west into this land called Arkansas, then later they were herded up and sent to the Indian Territory."

Thia's voice shook with anger. "And I'll tell you something else, Houston. Your namesake, Samuel Houston of Texas, considered himself a member of the Cherokee tribe. He *knew* what Andrew Jackson was doing to his people and he went to Washington, D.C., in full Cherokee dress to plead to the United States government for fairness for the Indian. You would do well to read his words concerning the injustice to the Indian and then dedicate your life to helping the Cherokee survive in this last wooded country that even now the whites are invading."

Houston flushed with anger and perhaps humiliation. "I'll do what I think is right but I don't need any of your history lessons, Miss Starr!"

After that, they rode on in silence. Ruff felt troubled and uncomfortable and wished he could think of some way to smooth things over between Thia and his brother. But Houston was in no mood for talk and he'd never admit to being wrong about anything because of his pride and stubbornness.

That night, they approached Fort Smith and knew they were almost at the western boundary of the Oklahoma Territory. They found that the fort had been captured by Union forces only a few months earlier.

"Unless there are strong objections, we'll circle around it under cover of darkness and enter the Indian Territory before daybreak," Houston said.

No one objected, and that long night they crossed into Oklahoma and passed into the heavy wooded country that marked the relocation of the Cherokee, Creek, Chickasaw, Choctaw, and Seminole, who were referred to as the Five Civilized Tribes of the South. The Cherokee were supposed to be in the northeastern corner of the Indian Territory, the Choctaw in the southeast, while most of the Creek, Chickasaw and Seminole were shoved in between and out to the western edge of the reservations lands.

None of the Indian tribes had wished to be located and all had suffered. Besides the Cherokee's Trail of Tears, where more than four thousand had died, out of one group of a thousand Choctaw, only eighty-eight had survived relocation. The Florida Seminoles had lived for years in the Everglades until finally, at the point of total annihilation by the United States Army, they were rounded up and driven to Oklahoma.

Ruff knew little more than this vague, skeletal outline of the tragic history of the Five Civilized Tribes. He had often listened to bigots speak of the red man as if they were animals that needed to be displaced far from the whites where they could be neither seen nor heard. The trouble was, the tide of white emigration kept pushing westward, and now the Indian Territory was being coveted by increasing numbers of whites.

There was another problem that Ruff hadn't understood and which even Thia didn't seem to know much about.

"It's the Plains Indians," she said sometime late that night as they rode under a canopy of cold stars. "They don't care that the United States government has carved out an Indian Territory. The Kiowa, and the Comanche are accustomed to living on horseback, and they will kill any intruders on their hunting grounds, which border the Indian Territory. That means that the so-called Five Civilized Tribes not only have to contend with a new home, but they have to protect it against fierce Plains Indians as well as a strengthening tide of whites."

Ruff shook his head. "Maybe we'd all be better to just go on to Texas. It sounds like we're riding into about as much trouble as we've left."

"Don't be talking such nonsense," Dixie said. "We were run out of Tennessee by the Union army after there was only the three of us left to carry on with father's line of horses and his dream. By coming here, we are joining our mother's people and making a stand."

Ruff hadn't quite thought of it that way, and when he glanced at Houston he could see that his brother hadn't, either. And though neither of them were disposed to admit that their fourteen-year-old smart-alecky sister ever made sense, there was something profound and true in her statement.

Ruff knew that he was tired of running. Tired of the Ballou name being vilified and slandered by Southerners because they had been forced to kill bad men who just happened to have been wearing Confederate uniforms. And if there were vengeance-minded men on their backtrail, then it would be better to make their stand sooner rather than later. And they'd do it in the Indian Territory, where the white man's law did not reign supreme.

"Are we coming to a town or what?" Houston grumbled. "These horses are about played out and I'm damned hungry and tired myself."

"There are towns everywhere in the Indian Territory but most of us consider them as villages," Thia informed them. "The important thing is that we all have Cherokee blood in our veins and we are in the Cherokee lands, where we will be welcomed and protected."

"I don't need any protection by Indians," Houston grumbled.

Thia started to say something but then, in the thin starlight, Ruff shook his head and Thia took his cue and held her tongue.

They were all so weary they were nearly falling out of their saddles when they made morning camp beside a pretty creek that flowed through a forest of what Thia called black jack oak. These trees were old and twisted but not especially tall. When Ruff laid his head down on his saddle after a breakfast of cold biscuits, fried pork, and strong coffee, he looked up and admired the unusual contortions of the twisted tree branches.

But then, with the sun struggled up to warm his face, he drifted off to sleep.

When he awoke, the sun was shafting light straight down through the overhead branches, and everyone was still napping. Ruff rolled to his feet and strapped on his six-gun before he went over to inspect the Thoroughbreds, the mules, and the eight horses they had captured back in Arkansas. All were fine but thin and listless.

Ruff walked over to the creek and washed his face, clearing his senses. He studied this new land, not finding it quite to his liking but not disliking it, either. Eastern Oklahoma appeared to be very much like the country that they had crossed in western Arkansas. There were forests separated by grass and meadowlands. The trees were of hickory, black jack oak, elms, and sycamores. Recent storms had left the ground moist and spongy and the taste of forest decay was sharp in Ruff's nostrils.

On impulse, he bridled a gelding and hopped on its bare back. He drummed his heels against the horse's ribs and sent it climbing up a steep game trail toward the crown of a domed limestone hill. Ruff felt good, and the undulating muscles of the gelding worked hard to carry them up to a burned-out area on the hilltop, where a bolt of lightning had splintered and charred a single oak tree. The earth was wet and black from soot and ash. Ruff slipped off the puffing gelding's back and tied the animal's reins to the oak's charred remains.

He thumbed back the brim of his hat and studied the vast forest panorama that flowed off in every direction. To the southwest, glinting like a silver thread, he saw what he supposed was the Arkansas River, into which all other rivers in this part of the country seemed to empty. Somewhere near its confluence with the Verdigris River rested Fort Gibson. Over it all floated a silent red-tailed hawk.

Ruff studied the hawk. Most Indians believed that the eagle and hawk were omens of good things, and Ruff hoped this one proved to be so for his exiled family and their famed Ballou Thoroughbreds. He recalled Thia explaining that this country was called the Ozark Plateau, and the Cherokee, after losing their homelands, were very glad to have received it from the United States government, for they considered this the most beautiful part of the Indian Territory.

Ruff could see why. In all directions he saw nothing but forest, which teemed with game pocketed everywhere by huge lakes and cut by winding rivers, some great but most small. In a valley Ruff judged to be less than ten miles to the west, he saw wavery columns of smoke rising toward a blue sky. It was there, Ruff reasoned, that either a town or a large village rested. Maybe Thia would know of its name.

The hawk wheeled suddenly and folded its wings and dived toward the earth. Ruff watched it disappear but his eyes remained pinned to the spot until, a moment later, the little hawk sailed back into the blue sky with something squirming in its talons. Even from such a distance, Ruff could hear the hawk's triumphant call as it glided toward a lofty oak dining table.

Ruff studied the forest, trying to gauge its mood and its promise for him and his life. It looked so serene and he knew he had to beware the temptation of allowing its outward appearance to seduce him into a false sense of security. The Civil War was still under way, thousands were still being slaughtered on battlefields, and the South would fight to the last measure of its being.

When Ruff thought of the war, he thought of little but death and destruction. He and Houston had been bought out of the Confederate army because their father had needed them at Wildwood Farm and also because old Justin had believed that losing three sons was price enough for any cause, even that of the South. Ruff and Houston, being the youngest sons, hadn't had any say in the matter, and there had been a thousand times when they'd both threatened to join the hemmorrhaging Confederate armies even if it meant defying their father.

But they hadn't, and despite the guilt Ruff felt about his passive role, he was also glad that he was still alive to carry on his father's work with the Thoroughbreds. To build something rather than to destroy.

"Ruff?"

He whirled, hand flashing to the Colt on his hip but then freezing on its walnut grip when he saw that it was Thia Starr. Unlike himself, Thia had climbed the hill on foot and now she was out of breath.

"Why didn't you hop on a pony?" he asked, relaxing with a smile of gentle amusement.

"I like to walk and the horses are so tired," Thia explained, coming to Ruff's side and leaning up against him just as if she had been doing that sort of thing for years. Just as if . . . as if they had been married and fitted for a long, long time.

Ruff draped an arm around her shoulders and studied the hazy blue-green forests, the lakes, and shiny rivers.

Thia looked up at him. "What do you think of the Indian Territory?"

He thought about that for a moment. Saw no reason to tell her that his heart was still in the Smoky Mountains of his homeland in Tennessee. "I think this is a very rich and fine country," he told her at last.

She turned slightly, face upraised as she looked deep into his eyes. "But it's not home, isn't that what you're thinking right now?"

"Yes," he admitted, for he had already learned he could not lie or hide his true feelings from Thia.

She sighed and frowned. Seemed to study hard on what she wanted to tell him. "Rufus, you—"

"Why did you call me Rufus just now?" he interrupted.

"Because sometimes, when you make things difficult for me, I think of you as a Rufus rather than a Ruff."

"Oh."

"Anyway, Rufus, you need to understand that home is a state of mind. It's not a place, but a . . . a feeling we have in our minds and our hearts. Home is where the heart is."

"Oh really?" he asked with a twinkle in his dark eyes.

"Yes! And don't you dare mock me. Your Cherokee have lost their traditional home, then been shuffled to Arkansas, and then to this Indian Territory. Every time it happened, they suffered and died. But each time, they gritted their teeth and started over."

The twinkle died. "And that's what you're telling me. That the Ballou family is just going to have to grit its teeth and start over."

"Yes. If you went back to Tennessee, Dixie has told me that you have so many enemies among both ex-Union soldiers as well as ex-Confederate soldiers, that you'd all be shot and killed if not hanged."

"Dixie told you that?"

"Yes. And she's terribly worried that Houston is going to go back and try to pick up the trail of Molly O'Day and that he'll be captured and executed if not ambushed."

Ruff considered that in grave silence and he had to agree with Dixie's somber assessment. "She's right," Ruff said, "but I know Houston better than she does and he's not going to be content for very long burying himself in this forest and grubbing out a livelihood."

"It wouldn't be 'grubbing,' " Thia argued. "There will be a cabin to build, barns to raise, pastures and fences to erect. And then an exercise track. The word about your horses will spread far beyond the Indian Territory until people come from all over the South again to buy, and breed their mares with your stallions."

"You make it sound so idyllic."

Thia kissed his whiskery cheek. "It will be good for us all this time," she promised. "We'll prosper here. I'm sure of it."

"I'm glad to hear that," Ruff said. He looked past the Cherokee girl toward the distant plumes of smoke. "Any idea who or what is causing that?"

"Of course! I've been here before, remember?"

"Well, then?"

"It's a Cherokee village. Or, if you prefer, a town of about a thousand people."

"Houston will want to buy some whiskey."

"There's none allowed in the territory. There are hard rules set by both the Cherokee and the United States government that say no whiskey in the Indian Territory."

Ruff shook his head. "Well, then that pretty well cinches the duck. Houston will never stand for that very long."

"He can ride fifty miles to the north and be out of the territory. He'll find dirty little settlements that are as rough as anything we saw in Arkansas. They exist for no other reason than to smuggle whiskey and sin into the Indian Territory."

"Whiskey and sin can appeal to some men," Ruff said darkly.

"But not to you," Thia said, a plea in her eyes.

Ruff studied her lovely, heart-shaped face and heard himself say, "No, not for me."

They kissed then and held each other tight against the backdrop of forest and sky. After a long while, Ruff grabbed Thia by the waist and swung her up onto the back of his gelding. Then, because he didn't want her to think he was anything but a horseman, he grabbed the horse's mane and swung up beside her.

Bareback and riding double, they traversed the crooked game trail back down to their camp by the cold forest stream.

EIGHT

The Cherokee town of Lockwood was far larger and more civilized than any of the Ballous had expected. In fact, aside from the fact that it was peopled mostly by Cherokee, only a few of whom were dressed in their tradition clothing of skins, moccasins, and leggings, it could well have been just another frontier settlement. The only real difference was that there were no saloons, gambling halls, or houses of prostitution so typical outside the territory.

The town even had its own newspaper, *The Lockwood Ledger*, written and printed in the Cherokee's own native written language, invented a little over forty years earlier by Sequoyah. Thia cajoled Ruff into buying a copy, and he could not make heads or tails of it, and neither could Houston or Dixie.

"It's easy to read," Thia told them. "It uses a syllabary of eighty-six characters that reflect all the sounds of our spoken language. Even children can learn it in a week or two."

Ruff raised his eyebrows and then Thia turned the paper over to reveal that the news had been reprinted in English on the back side of the paper.

"It's the way of things among our people," Thia explained with an impish grin. "We don't agree on much of anything. General Stand Watie is fighting for the Confederacy while others of the people are fighting for the Union."

"The Union!" Houston growled. "Now why the hell would they do that!"

"For the very same reasons that Aunt Margaret understood so well. They believe the Union will win and they don't want to be punished by the victors when the war finally ends."

Houston snorted something in anger and gazed up and down the street lined with businesses. "If this don't beat all," he said. "You can buy anything but fun in this sorry town."

"If that means bad whiskey and even worse women," Dixie scolded, "then I'm all for it."

"Isn't there anything to drink in this place?"

"Water," Thia said with obvious disapproval. "But in truth, there's always bootleg liquor to be had if you've got to drink the Devil's brew."

"Well," Houston bristled, "I don't 'got' to do anything. But I reckon that I like to decide when and where I can wet my whistle without asking anyone's permission!"

Ruff steered his brother off on another subject. "I guess we need to talk to someone about filing for a section of land to build on."

"There is a Cherokee lawyer just up the street," Thia said, remounting her horse. "He probably handles all that kind of thing."

Houston drove the wagon on down the avenue with the Ballou Thoroughbreds, attracting a good deal more attention than their owners. They passed a Baptist and a Methodist church, a schoolyard filled with Cherokee children at play, and stores of every description except the common and ever-present Western saloon.

"I'll rust away like a piece of old machinery in this Indian Territory," Houston muttered. "A man has got to have some inner lubrication now and again."

Ruff and Dixie exchanged worried glances. Houston could be mighty cantankerous when he wanted something he could not have.

"How far is it to the nearest border and white town?" Houston demanded.

"Sixty miles as the crow flies," Thia said.

"When our horses get rested, that's just one good day's run," Houston said.

Ruff started to argue that fact but Thia took his arm and led him on down the street with Houston, still muttering his displeasure. They entered a small but orderly office and interrupted a scholarly-looking man who was reading the *Lockwood Ledger*.

The man peeked over a pair of wire-rimmed spectacles and said, "My name is Jackson J. Rattlinggourd, attorney at law. Can I help you folks?"

Houston was still too angry to be civil, so Ruff answered. "We've just arrived from Tennessee and are looking to settle in the Indian Territory."

Lawyer Rattlinggourd studied them with heightened interest. He was short, plump, and in his late forties. His black hair was shot with silver and he had thick, bushy eyebrows, a hooked nose, and intense but not threatening black eyes. When he arose from his desk and bumped across his office floor, Ruff could see that he had a bad leg that gave him a pronounced limp.

"How much blood?" Rattlinggourd asked.

"Huh?"

Thia linked her arm through Ruff's. "I'm a half-blood. I belong to the Starr family."

"I can see you're at least half-blood," the lawyer said. "It's these other folks that I'm not so sure about."

"We're quarter-bloods," Ruff said, feeling as if his ancestry had just been questioned. "Is that good enough?"

"Of course!" Rattlinggourd shook hands all around, and then he went back to the comfort of his desk and chair. "But I'll need some proof. We've too many whites coming in here just saying that they are part Cherokee in order to get the rights to settle on our lands. Either that, or they pay some poor Cherokee girl's family a bunch of gold to marry her. If a white marries a Cherokee, they can claim land."

"He's going to marry me someday," Thia said, giving Ruff's arm a squeeze. "Maybe he'll marry me right now if that's what it takes."

"Now wait a minute!" Ruff objected. "I don't mean to get rushed into a thing that important."

Dixie stepped up before Rattlinggourd's battered oaken desk and reached into her coat pocket. "I brought these letters," she said. "I've carried them all the way from Tennessee and they are to and from my mother to her Cherokee people, some of whom are still living in North Carolina."

Rattlinggourd nodded and took the letters. "Do these contain references to you and your brothers in respect to your Cherokee ancestry?"

"Of course," Dixie said, untying a ribbon that bound the letters in a piece of soft doeskin.

"Would you look at that!" Ruff said, surprised and delighted by his sister.

Houston wasn't impressed. He didn't look as if he gave a tinker's damn whether or not they were accepted as mixed-bloods and given the right to settle in the Indian Territory. As a matter of fact, he glared with irritation at the letters.

"I'll need to go over the letters to be sure they are legitimate," Rattlinggourd explained. "Unless you wish to read only the pertinent references aloud to me in private."

Houston scoffed. "Oh, for hell sakes! We aren't applying for a rich mining claim in the middle of the Comstock Lode! There's more land in this territory than you and all the Indians will ever farm."

"You're wrong about that," the Cherokee lawyer replied, not the least bit perturbed by Houston's abrupt behavior. "We've plenty of fine open land good for farms or cattle raising. That's why we must be very careful about who is allowed in to settle. The Indian Territory is our last refuge from injustice, Mr. Ballou."

Rattlinggourd paused and his black eyes hardened just a measure. "As refugees yourselves from the heart of Dixie, I would think you'd finally be able to appreciate why we intend to husband our reservation land so zealously."

The muscles stretched across Houston's cheeks but when he spoke, his voice was much calmer and more respectful. "Yes, I guess maybe I do understand, sir."

"Mr. Rattlinggourd, we're not farmers or cattle ranchers. What we want to do is raise Thoroughbred racing horses."

The lawyer smiled. He had a round, pleasant face and now he filled it with a brier pipe whose stem he sucked on without the bother of tobacco. "It'll be ideal for your Thoroughbreds but we've already got some mighty fine ones in the territory. Nothing brings us Indians out on a Sunday faster than the prospect of a good horse race."

Houston brightened. "We've got the finest that ever entered this territory. We're the Ballous of Tennessee."

The lawyer shrugged. "By your tone of voice, I gather that means something in Tennessee, Mr. Ballou, but it cuts no ice in this pond."

Houston chuckled. "If there is to be horse racing in this part of your territory, it'll cut a lot of ice before we move on to greener pasters."

"Are you really a lawyer?" Dixie asked, going over to stare at a framed diploma hanging on the wall.

"From Princeton," Rattlinggourd said with pride. "My family was blessed with good business skills and owned a very large plantation in Arkansas. When we were forced to leave, they were able to sell many of the assets and bring in one last bumper crop of tobacco. I've been blessed with a good deal of opportunity and I've tried to repay it to our people."

Rattlinggourd puffed up a little. "I'm not ashamed to tell you that I've an auditorium at the missionary school in Tahlequah named after me because of my financial support. And, if your horse-racing enterprise proves to be successful, you can count on my soliciting you to support that same worthy educational establishment."

Ruff stifled a grin. Cherokee or no Cherokee, this man's choice of ten-dollar words branded him as a slightly overeducated lawyer from a big-name eastern college. Rattlinggourd didn't need a framed diploma to convince Ruff of his legal credentials.

Ruff was about to ask the lawyer a question when, quite suddenly, Rattlinggourd paled and seemed to shiver. He removed the cigar from his mouth and jumped to his feet. For a moment, he closed his eyes and gripped the edge of his desk. When he opened his eyes, Ruff said, "Are you all right, sir?"

"Not really," the lawyer said, staring past them through his office window at the street where there was some kind of commotion.

Thia and the Ballous turned around and stared, too. They saw a knot of people growing into a crowd as it surrounded a young man and what appeared to be his pregnant wife. They were sitting in a buckboard. The wife's head was bowed and covered with her brown hands. It was obvious that she was distraught.

"What's the matter?" Dixie asked.

For a moment, Rattlinggourd was unable to answer. Then he said, "It's Abraham Sixkiller and he's decided it's time."

"For what!" Thia asked as the lawyer composed himself and went over to a hatrack for his derby.

Rattlinggourd paused. "I guess you might as well have it explained by me as someone who might have the facts twisted. I represented young Abraham six months ago in our Cherokee capital of Tahlequah, where he was arrested and charged with murdering a mixed-blood who was sympathetic to the Union. You see, Abraham Sixkiller has ridden with General Stand Watie's Confederate cavalry."

"He killed another man over this war?" Houston scoffed. "Mr. Rattlinggourd, that's not so unusual a crime in these bloody times."

"Perhaps not, but we have our own Cherokee laws based on a Constitution very much like that of the United States. There was little I could do because Abraham Sixkiller attacked the victim and stabbed him to death during the argument. And now he's come to fulfill his death sentence."

"What?"

Rattlinggourd placed his hat on his head and looked in a mirror to straighten his tie. "He needed some time to get his affairs in order. Apparently, he's done that and now he's come to die."

Houston shook his head, still not comprehending. "You mean he and his wife just drive in here and hand themselves over to die?"

"Yes."

"But . . . he killed a Yankee lover!"

"He broke the Cherokee law!" Rattlinggourd snapped. "He gave his word of honor that he'd come when his affairs were in order—and he has."

Houston looked at the others. "Can you believe this?"

"Yes," Thia said. "It is a matter of Cherokee honor. He had no choice but to come for his execution."

"He could have run! Could have saved his life! What . . . ?"

"Where could a full-blood run to?" Thia asked. "Without his own people and traditions, he would already be dead. This way, he redeems himself. A Cherokee's honor is no less than any other Southerner's."

Houston was brought up short. He jammed his hands into his pants and his face was grim. "Hey, Rattlinggourd," he called as the attorney started out the front door, "what are they going to do, hang him?"

"Firing squad at sundown," the lawyer said as he headed for the condemned man and his pregnant wife.

Ruff looked at Thia, then Dixie, and finally his brother. Like them, he was shocked that a man would voluntarily come in to be executed. Not many whites would do so just to preserve their way of honor. But on the other hand, Ruff felt he kind of understood Thia's meaning that a full-blood Cherokee like Sixkiller really had no place to run. Sixkiller wore the old traditional Cherokee buckskins and leggings. You only had to look at the proud set of his chin and the way he held himself to realize that although he wasn't much older than Ruff, he was very proud.

"I don't want to watch this," Thia said to Ruff. "Can we go for a walk at sundown?"

"Sure." Ruff turned to his sister and brother. "Why don't you both join us?"

Dixie nodded but Houston shook his head. "I'll watch," he said. "Courage and honor demand my attendance."

"All right," Ruff said, taking the girl's arms and heading outside to skirt the upset and gathering crowd of mostly Indians.

At sundown, the three of them heard the volley of a firing squad. Thia's body stiffened and her face was as lovely and brittle as chinaware. Dixie hugged one of the Thoroughbred mares and cried.

"We'll make camp out here tonight," Ruff said in the falling darkness when he saw Houston approach from the town. "I don't think Mr. Rattlinggourd will be of a mind to help us file a land claim today."

That evening around their campfire, the mood was somber and there was very little talk. The weather had moderated and there was no wind to cut through the trees.

Houston finished off the last of his liquor but it wasn't very much. After that, he sat staring into the flames, his expression morose and troubled. Finally, he said, "Sixkiller died well. The firing squad did clean work."

"What about Mrs. Sixkiller?" Thia asked.

"She watched."

Ruff shook his head.

"There was almost another killing just before the execution," Houston said. He waited a moment, then added, "Between the Unionists and those loyal to the Confederacy."

"What . . . ?"

"There were enough of us to stop it," Houston interrupted, without adding any elaboration.

Ruff glanced at Dixie, who just shrugged. Like Ruff, she would have assumed that Houston, if he had become involved at all, would have sided with those Cherokee sympathetic to the Confederacy. The idea that he had actually intervened and prevented bloodshed was surprising.

Houston removed his hat and ran his long, supple fingers through his hair. When he spoke, it was not to them but to the fire . . . or perhaps to himself. He sounded as if he were trying to convince a disbeliever of his words.

"It just seemed . . . well," he struggled, "it just seemed as if more blood was shed, then Sixkiller would have been dishonored. I mean . . . isn't that *why* the man came back?"

Ruff reached out and patted Houston on the shoulder.

"Yeah," he said, "that's exactly why he must have come back."

"Son of a bitch," Houston hissed at the fire before he climbed heavily to his feet and walked off into the night.

Ruff watched his brother disappear and he had about decided to go after him and offer solace when Dixie said, "Let him alone, Ruff."

"But . . ."

"She's right," Thia said.

"What makes you both think that you understand him better than I do!" Ruff snapped, eyes flashing in the firelight as he turned from one to the other.

Neither Thia nor Dixie had an answer, but Ruff stayed put until the fire died, and then he went to his blankets.

Much, much later Houston returned and bedded down. Ruff looked over and whispered, "You all right, brother?"

"Yeah."

"Want to talk?"

"No."

"Okay."

Ruff closed his eyes and wished for sleep. And for Tennessee yesterdays. But most of all, he wished for an end to all the suffering and the dying.

NINE

Ruff, Dixie, Thia, and Houston spent almost three weeks riding through empty sections of the Indian Territory seeking just the right piece of land for their horse ranch. Most of the meadowlands they came upon simply weren't big enough for the pastures, barns, corrals, and racetrack they intended to build. Or, if they were large enough, they rested on a slope making them unfit for a racetrack. Ruff had no intention of grading down a track, and so he kept searching. Each new unsettled valley he came upon filled him with initial hope but then proved disappointing. Their search finally brought them to what was considered to be the very northern boundaries of the Indian Territory.

"This is almost Kansas," Ruff said, studying a rough map that Mr. Rattlinggourd had given him. "Kansas has sided with the Union, and I'll be damned if I want to live near 'em."

Houston was passionate in his agreement. "They don't call it 'Bleeding Kansas' for nothing. Our Captain Quantrill sure showed them Yankee lovers the error of their ways."

William C. Quantrill, a ruthless and daring Confederate captain, had led a daring and bloody raid on Lawrence, Kansas, the summer before in which his raiders had left 150 dead and the town a smoldering ruins. When Ruff looked north into Kansas Territory, he had a bad feeling in his gut that told him it would be foolish to build so close to that war-torn country.

"Let's circle around and follow the Verdegris River south again," Ruff suggested, reining High Fire up and standing in his stirrups.

"Land along that river is likely to be already taken," Houston argued.

"I don't think so. Most of the Cherokee are located southeast of us, over near their capital at Tahlequah and Fort Gibson. I think we've about got our pick of this part of the territory."

"We aren't going to do much horse business if we're stuck out here away from anyone and everyone," Houston said, not pleased by the idea of living on the fringe of both the white and the Indian Territory.

"That's a good point," Dixie said.

Ruff glanced at Thia and the Cherokee girl wisely held her thoughts in private. If he had to take a guess, Ruff imagined that Thia would also have preferred to live closer to the main Cherokee populations. This country, while beautiful and almost empty, free for their taking, could get lonely and no doubt was at the mercy of raiders, both Union and Confederate. It might also attract Plains Indians, such as the fast-moving and deadly Kiowa, who had already staged many bloody raids on the Five Civilized Tribes.

Ruff was just about to touch his heels to his stallion's flanks when he saw a movement down in the low valley beyond. "Look, see them!"

Houston nodded and wheeled High Man around and galloped into the cover of trees with everyone following. They dismounted and tied their horses, then studied the riders who were still about a half mile away but coming along at a steady trot. There were seven heavily armed riders escorting five prisoners. It was easy to see that they were prisoners because their hands were tied behind their backs and their horses were yoked to those of their captors.

"What do you make of it?" Ruff asked.

Nobody knew what to think. A posse? A group of regulators or a vigilante committee?

"They don't look like soldiers," Dixie said. "Neither Rebs or Yanks."

"You can't be sure of that," Ruff said. "With the war damn near lost, there are people on both sides that are raiding and plundering. There's no civil law to speak of anymore."

"There is in the Indian Territory," Thia interrupted. "And that might just be the Cherokee Lighthorse Police."

"The what?"

"The Lighthorse," Thia repeated. "I've never seen them and they usually don't travel in such a large group but I'll bet that's what they are."

"If so, why are they riding north instead of heading for Tahlequah?"

Thia had a ready explanation. "They'd be escorting whites off the Indian land."

"For what reason?" Houston wanted to know.

"For running liquor, mostly. Or for trying to rob and cheat our people or just for raising the devil," Thia explained.

"Why don't they sentence them or hand them over to the white authorities?"

"I don't know."

Houston remounted. "Maybe I'll go down and find out."

"Houston, no!" Ruff said angrily. "Whatever they're up to, it's none of our business."

"Maybe not," Houston said, "but I'm bored damn near into senility. I need some excitement."

Dixie looked to Ruff to stop their brother but Ruff just shrugged and then he untied High Fire and swung into his own saddle. "I guess I'd better tag along. You girls best stay here until—"

"Not a chance!" Dixie swore, and Thia let it be known she was of the same mind.

Ruff touched heels to flanks and raced after his brother. This made damn poor sense but he wasn't about to hide while Houston went down and found out who those men were and what they were doing with prisoners.

When the seven horsemen saw the Ballous racing toward them, they yanked their rifles, jumped off their horses, and used the animals for cover. Houston and Ruff suddenly found themselves galloping straight into a forest of the rifle sights and it wasn't a good feeling.

They drew their Thoroughbred stallions up sharply and raised their right hands to indicate that their intentions were peaceable. For almost a minute, the seven armed Cherokee stared at them over their saddles and then one of them motioned them forward.

"I told you we should have stayed the hell back in the trees and let this pass us by," Ruff growled.

But Houston didn't hear him or, if he did, paid Ruff no mind. Houston looked almost happy and there was a grin on his face. "This ought to be right interesting," he said as he rode forward toward the nest of rifles.

Ruff swore to himself and followed his brother. Closer inspection left no doubt that the armed men were Cherokee. Most of them wore the Indian trappings. Black, flat-brimmed hats, an eagle or hawk's feather in the hatband, and moccassins. All had black eyes and dark, guarded expressions.

The leader of the Cherokee detached from the circle of protection and laid his rifle across his chest. His six men stayed within the circle of horses watching Ruff, Houston, and the approaching girls as well as their white prisoners.

"Good afternoon!" Houston said, drawing his horse up and tipping his own hat. "We are scouting for land up in this part of the country and happened to see you men. We were just wondering what it was that you were up to."

Ruff groaned low in his throat. Even to him, the excuse sounded flimsy and foolish. The Cherokee leader was a large man who appeared to be in his late thirties. His dark complexion told Ruff that he was mostly Indian, if not actually a full-blood.

"Who are you?" the Indian leader demanded.

Houston introduced himself, Ruff, and then Dixie and Thia. When the leader did not smile or show any outward friendliness, Houston glanced at Ruff, who looked right through his brother. He was furious at Houston who had gotten them into this serious mess and would now have to talk them out of it.

"Thia?" Houston asked hopefully. "Wasn't it you that thought these ... gentlemen might be members of the Cherokee Lighthorse Police?"

"That's right," Thia said.

"They're a bunch of bloody sons a bitches, is all they are," one of the prisoners swore. "They ain't got no right to beat the hell out of us and drag us halfway across this territory!"

Ruff had not dared to take his eyes off the Indians and really study the prisoners, but he did so now. And he was shocked. All five of the men had obviously been beaten, and most had swollen faces and black eyes. But then, now that he really looked at the Cherokee, he could see that one had been shot and two more were also badly injured. One had his arm in a sling and another had a head wound with a bloody turban for a bandage.

"This is Indian Territory, white men," the leader said bluntly. "Ride out of it."

"Now wait a minute," Houston said. "We're part Indian ourselves. A quarter Cherokee."

The leader stared at them. Their black eyes and hair raised a doubt in his mind. "Your names?"

"We're are the Ballous of Tennessee."

"That's not a Cherokee name."

"Our mother was Lucinda Eldee Starr. She was a half-blood," Dixie said, then added quickly, "Mr. Jackson J. Rattlinggourd has the letters to prove this. He told us there was free land we could claim up in this part of the Indian Territory."

Hope died in the prisoners' eyes. They could see that the Ballous would not help them. One of the prisoners screwed up his face and stared at Thia. "Little woman," he said in a hard, mean voice, "you just settle into this lonesome country up here. We'll be back soon and I'll pay you a little visit some night when ..."

Ruff drew his six-gun and before anyone could react, he fired. The man's hat sailed off his head and his jaw dropped.

"I think you'd better watch your mouth, mister," Ruff said, not holstering his six-gun but keeping it aimed at the prisoner, who finally had the presence of mind to close his gaping mouth.

"My name is Tobacco John," the leader said, spitting a stream of tobacco to the earth. "We belong to the Lighthorse and we're taking these men back across the border. We caught them trying to steal Indian cattle."

"Hell, we weren't stealing anything!" one of the prisoners shouted. "We was just driving 'em along, looking for where they belonged and hoping a good deed would earn us a few steaks, that's all."

Houston said, "That kind of wishful behavior will get you strung up in most parts of the country. You're lucky that all that happened to you was that you got whipped. In most places, you'd be candidates for a noose party."

"We caught them once before," the leader said. "My name is Sergeant Bluford West, or just plain Blue."

Blue introduced the others members of his Lighthorse.

"You've got some men that have been shot," Ruff said with some concern.

"They'll be all right," Blue said. "Besides, they wouldn't return to Tahlequah and leave us out in this country. Not until we've taken these prisoners across the line and turned them loose."

"Turned them loose?" Houston asked. "But that doesn't make any sense! If these men were breaking the law and they shot some of your Lighthorse, then . . ."

Blue West shrugged. "I guess that Rattlinggourd didn't explain the facts of life in the Indian Territory."

"No," Houston said, "we talked about land rights, not criminal rights."

Blue dismounted and ordered his men to lead their horses and the prisoners over to a nearby stream.

"How about untying our wrists so we can drink like white men!" snarled the same prisoner whose hat Ruff had ventilated.

Blue's eyes narrowed and a vein throbbed in his forehead. "Get down on your knees in the mud and lap the water up like the stinking coyotes you and your cutthroats are, Harlan."

Harlan muttered a curse and Blue turned his back on the man and managed a thin smile, but the vein in his forehead was still distended and pulsing.

"Why don't we walk a little upstream," Blue said, "where we can talk without being overheard."

Ruff, Dixie, Thia, and Houston all followed the Cherokee Lighthorse sergeant a few hundred feet until they came to a nice sunny place to drink and relax. Ruff noticed that Blue put his back against a sycamore tree so that he could watch the prisoners and his men and that the Cherokee's hand never strayed very far from the worn butt of his six-gun.

"Harlan and this bunch are a bad lot," Blue said with a weary shake of his head. "This is the third time we've had to bring him out of the Indian Territory, and it was all that I could do to keep my men from stringing the lot of them up from a tall tree."

"Maybe you should have," Houston drawled, his eyes also on the prisoners. "So, why didn't you?"

"We can't," Blue said. "Jackson Rattlinggourd should have explained to you that because we are the Indian Nation, our laws have no jurisdiction over intruders."

"Even those that break the law?"

"That's right." Blue sighed. "Oh, we can take them over to Fort Smith and ask Hanging Judge Parker to charge them, but how do we prove our charges? And sometimes we've had to stay around as witnesses for months while the accused's attorney plays games. We can't afford to do that, so the charges are often dropped for lack of evidence."

"That sounds like a real mess," Houston said with genuine sympathy.

"It is," Blue said. "Mostly we just evict white squatters or those trying to steal our grass, timber, or minerals. But sometimes we get some real bad ones like this bunch."

"Shoot them," Ruff said.

Blue chuckled to himself. He picked a dead stem of grass and poked it between his lips. He chewed thoughtfully and said, "We've strung up and shot a few. Sometimes they won't go out of this territory any way except feetfirst and we'll accomodate them. Trouble is, if the United States Army catches wind of the fact, we're in deep trouble. They send in investigators, and being white . . ."

Blue didn't say any more. He didn't have to. After a long silence, Houston said, "How much time do you and your men spend in the saddle?"

"Most of it," Blue said. "Too damn much. It's hard to find Indians willing to make the kind of sacrifices that are needed. Most of my men are Cherokee full-bloods. But we welcome mixed-bloods and members of the other tribes. The man with the head wound, for example, is Creek. That fella in the old army coat with the red bandanna around his throat is a Chickasaw."

"And you get along?" Ruff asked.

"We have no choice. We ride over all the Indian Territory, not just the Cherokee parts. One of our biggest headaches is the whiskey and rum runners. They just keep bringing it in and we keep trying to stop it. But hell," Blue conceded, "it's like trying to put your finger in a dike."

"I'll bet," Houston said, licking his lips. "I thirst for some whiskey myself."

Blue looked amused. "I probably shouldn't tell you this, but now and then, me and the boys have been known to sample a bottle or two—just to make sure that it really is bootleg whiskey, you understand."

Houston chuckled. "Yeah, I understand."

"We're looking for a place to build a horse ranch in these parts," Dixie said, not interested in the matter of legal or illegal whiskey.

Blue's eyes shifted to Dixie and then to Thia. Finally, he studied the Ballou Thoroughbreds. "Yeah," he said. "I can see why. They look to be fine running animals."

"There are few better," Houston said. "The stallion I'm riding is seventeen, but he'll still outrun almost anything you've ever seen on four legs."

"How's his wind?" Blue asked. "In this country, endurance and soundness is more important than pure, blazing speed."

"He'll run from here to Tennessee and back without breaking stride," Houston said. "Never had a lame day in his life."

"He's had a few," Dixie said, not wanting Sergeant West to think that they were a bragging family.

"Damn few," Houston said.

"I sure wish we had a few horses like that," Blue West said wistfully. "Maybe someday. Right now, ours are played out, same as my men. I'd send the Creek and a couple of others back if I could, but there's no telling what we might meet up with along the border."

"What's to keep Harlan and his boys from just coming back a day after you turn them loose?"

Blue looked away for a moment. "We'll take their horses and keep them to cover our expenses. They raise hell about that sort of thing and have even sent soldiers down into our country to retrieve them but they never are found."

Blue winked. "But Harlan will come back again, and I expect we'll have to kill him the next time before he kills us. He and his boys are bad ones and they've sworn to take our lives the next time."

"I'd put the bastard out of his misery right now," Houston said, face hardening. "It sounds like the prudent thing to do."

Blue smiled wearily. "I wish you were my commanding officer. I like your way of thinking."

Houston frowned and Ruff knew from his brother's expression that Houston was coming to some kind of decision.

"Maybe if I tagged along," Houston said, not looking at Dixie or Ruff, "you could send the wounded back to get doctoring."

"You want to ride with the Cherokee Lighthorse?" Blue West asked with surprise.

"Beats riding around in circles looking for a place to nest. Ruff and Dixie can do that just fine without my help."

"Houston?" Ruff said. "I'm not sure that—"

"It's all right," Houston growled.

Blue was interested. "Can you shoot as quick and straight as your brother did a few minutes ago, when he sent Harlan's hat sailing from his head?"

Houston had been sitting down but now he stood up and pivoted around. There was a sapling about as big around as a man's forearm some thirty yards away. Houston's hand slapped leather and up came his gun. The Colt in his fist bucked five times so fast that the shots sort of rolled up like the tobacco leaves in a good Carolina cigar, tight and all together. The sapling broke at the center, white wood splinters flung in all directions.

Houston grinned and blew the smoke from his gun, then reloaded and holstered the weapon. "Is that good enough, Sergeant?"

Blue nodded. "It's better than any of the rest of us can shoot, but not by much. You'll do fine, Private Ballou."

Houston chuckled. "Private, huh?"

"That's right. You'll take orders from me and you'll take them without question. There'll be no discussions. Our lives depend on each other. When we get to the border, there's a town there called Lynchville."

"Nice name," Thia said cryptically.

"It fits the citizenry," Blue said. "The town is nothing but a nest of thieves, killers, and army deserters. They're all looking to prey off the Indian people down in our country. Mostly, they steal Indian cattle, although they also like to steal white man's cattle and try to make it look like it was the Cherokee people."

"I see." Houston rubbed his hands together briskly. "Well, I hope I get the chance to make their acquaintances."

Ruff thought it remarkable how interested in things Houston had suddenly become. For the last three weeks, he'd been withdrawn and seemingly uninterested in the location of their new horse ranch. His mind had been much on Molly O'Day or some other issue. Now, however, this chance meeting with the Cherokee Lighthorse seemed to have brought his older brother back to life.

Blue stretched. He was of medium height and he smelled of smoke and horse. When he moved, he moved like a man who had been in the saddle too long without rest. He moved like an old man.

Blue West said, "My men will show you a few places on the way back toward Tahlequah that will probably suit your needs as a horse ranch. I'll tell them what you are looking for and why. I'll also tell them that, someday, the Cherokee Lighthorse might be able to wangle a horse or two out of you in turn for the favor."

Ruff looked at Dixie and Houston. When neither of them objected to the possibility, he nodded. "Fair enough."

It took only a few minutes for everyone to remount and for the farewells to be made.

"You be careful and don't get yourself in trouble," Ruff said to his brother. He tried to make the statement in a joking manner, but it didn't work. Houston didn't appreciate being told anything, and now was no exception.

"Ruff, you just get to building if you find the right place. I'll be along directly."

"Fair enough."

Harlan couldn't resist a parting shot. He'd been allowed to retrieve his bullet-punctured hat and he glared at Ruff with pure hatred. "You folks just threw in with the wrong side and you'll come to regret that decision."

"Is that a warning?" Ruff asked in a dead-quiet voice.

"You damn right! You're more white blood than Indian blood. You didn't have to join these Cherokee bastards. I'll see you again, kid."

"I can hardly wait," Ruff said. "Next time, I'll aim about a foot lower."

Harlan blinked and then he and his tethered horse were led away. Ruff stayed and watched the Cherokee Lighthorse until they topped a rise and then disappeared. He found it difficult to believe that his brother had actually volunteered to ride with the Indians. Houston had always shown less interest in his Indian heritage than any of the rest of the family. He favored his father, in looks, style, and temperment. But now suddenly, he was riding off with the Indian police.

"He'll be fine," Thia said, riding up beside Ruff. "Your brother needs them more than they need him."

"How do you figure that?"

"It shows," Thia said without further elaboration.

Ruff puzzled on that one for a moment and then looked at the pair of wounded Lighthorse and knew it was time to find the nearest doctor.

TEN

Riding stirrup to stirrup with Sergeant Blue West of the Cherokee Lighthorse, Houston felt reborn. He felt light and yet strong with every sense tingling with life. After weary weeks of scouring the Indian Territory, looking at one potential homesteading site after another and always finding fault with them, now he was riding into Kansas and maybe into one hell of a good fight.

It wasn't that Houston wanted to kill or be killed, it was that, since saying good-bye to Molly O'Day with the strong likelihood he'd never see her again, he'd felt dead inside. He'd tried to bury his anger at losing his older brothers and his father, and then Wildwood Farm. Burying hadn't worked and neither had the whiskey he'd been able to drink until he'd run out of it in this Indian Territory. But now, clear eyed and with High Man running strong between his legs, Houston knew that danger and excitement was the only medicine that made any real sense for him. A man couldn't predict how life might change for him. All he could do was to take each day and live it to the fullest. Too long had Houston been wallowing in self-pity and boredom. Now he was riding into danger and he felt very, very good.

"How far is the border!" he called over to Blue.

The Cherokee raised a brown hand and pointed to a low rise of land just ahead. "That's the border."

"Where is Lynchville?"

"Right on the border. About twenty miles to the east."

"We going into Kansas?"

In answer, Blue reined his horse hard to the left and they left a dirt track they had been following and angled off to the west. Houston didn't understand what Blue West was up to, but he did know that he admired and respected the Cherokee as much as anyone he'd met in a long, long time. In the less than two days they'd ridden together, Houston had seen how a leader of men acted. Blue led by example. He didn't yell or threaten anyone. His orders, which were very few and always given in a soft but firm tone of voice, were quickly carried out.

Blue asked for no privileges of rank and, in fact, seemed inclined to work harder than any of his Lighthorse. He was also the most vigilant. His black eyes were never still and, somehow, he seemed completely oblivious of the cursing and scorn being constantly heaped upon him by his white captives.

Had Houston, who was at least ten years Blue's junior, have been subjected to that kind of verbal abuse, he would have lost his temper and either killed or beaten Harlan into silence. But Blue just took it as stoically as if he were a dumb animal and the abusive words were nothing but warm rain washing off his hide.

At first, this had bothered Houston and lessened the Cherokee in his eyes, but that thinking had quickly evaporated, replaced with understanding and respect.

One had to respect all these Lighthorse. From what Houston had learned, theirs was an almost impossible job—to control the white lawbreakers without any legal authority to mete out punishment.

"We've got to cross the border before we turn them loose," Blue explained. "And we want to be far enough from Lynchville that we aren't seen and that these men will have a nice long walk to reflect upon the sinfulness of their ways."

"You sons a bitches had better stick back to back like paper cutouts," Harlan shouted. "Because you're all dead men the next time we meet. Especially you, West!"

Houston longed to plant his knuckles through Harlan's yellow teeth but he kept his silence. This was the Lighthorse's affair and he was just helping them out to relieve his own acute case of boredom.

When Blue West had determined that they were well across the Kansas border, he drew rein and raised his arm in the air as a signal. The Lighthorse and their prisoners stopped and the Indians dismounted.

"Ride is over," Blue said, drawing his pistol and using it to gesture Harlan and his men down from their horses.

Harlan was in a rage. Despite his hands being bound behind his back, he actually appeared ready to lower his head and charge Blue. And maybe he would have if one of the Lighthorse had not had a firm grip on the back of his shirt.

"You sons a bitches ain't going to steal our horses and weapons this time, damn you!"

The Indian behind Harlan leaned back, planted his moccasin in the small of Harlan's back and shoved hard, sending the outlaw leader stumbling forward.

"Walk!" Blue ordered.

But Harlan had recovered his balance and whirled. "You're all dead men! All of you!"

Houston had never let any man threaten his life before and he saw no use in doing so now. He started forward but Blue caught his arm and shook his head. "Get back on your horse."

Houston was two inches taller than Blue and a far bigger man but something in the Cherokee's eyes made him turn and remount.

The Lighthorse wheeled their horses and those of the white men and began to ride slowly away. Houston was in the rear and he could hear the shouts and curses of the men they had left behind. Then suddenly, and to Houston's amazement and shock, a pistol exploded behind them, and this was followed by a second shot.

Blue cried out something and reined his horse around, his rifle coming up. One of the Lighthorse pitched from his mount, blood gushing from a hole in his back. Houston drew his six-gun even as the Cherokee screamed in rage and sent their horses racing at Harlan and his men. No one knew how Harlan had gotten hold of a weapon but it must have been hidden someplace on one of the prisoners.

Blue West raised his carbine and began to fire at the whites who whirled and scattered, running for their lives. The Lighthorse went after them like a fox after hens. Houston shot one runner in the arm and before he could fire again, one of the Lighthorse had drilled the man dead center. There were screams, and when Harlan collapsed to his knees, still trying to fire, Houston saw Blue leap from his horse, draw his knife, and attack. Harlan screamed and the hammer of his gun clicked on an empty cylinder just before Blue grabbed him by the hair and slit his throat.

Houston reined High Man up sharply and dismounted. He looked around just in time to see the last surviving prisoner die at the hands of the enraged Lighthorse. The entire bloody affair had lasted only a minute, maybe not even that long.

Blue West was gray faced as he walked back to the downed Indian. He knelt beside the man but he was already dead.

"My fault," Blue whispered bitterly. "We should have waited until they had walked away and only then turned our backs on them!"

"Any idea where the gun was hidden?" Houston asked.

Blue shook his head in reply. He looked old and sick at heart. Just looking at the tragic expression he wore made Houston want to turn away.

"What are we going to do, Sergeant?" one of the Indians asked. "If they're found, you know what will happen to the People."

"I know."

Blue stood up and pressed his thumbs to his temples. He shook his head as if locked in a nightmare. Houston looked to the other Indians to comfort the man but they also seemed paralyzed with grief.

"Look," Houston said quietly, "I'm sorry about Osceola. He was a good man, but what happened is no one's fault and it couldn't be helped."

"Houston?"

"Yes?"

Blue looked through him. "Don't say anything more, all right?"

"All right," Houston said, turning back to High Man and making a big thing out of checking his cinch and then reloading his pistol.

After a few minutes, Blue grabbed Osceola and, without any help, managed to get the man's body draped across his horse. Houston waited to see what the Lighthorse were going to do about the dead whites. His guess was that they'd be taken back into Indian Territory and buried in the forest where they'd likely never be found.

That seemed to be the course of events when Harlan and his companions were loaded on their horse and led back across the border.

"Since we haven't any shovels we had better look for some real soft earth to dig in," Houston said to no one in particular.

"We're not going to bury them," Blue said in a low voice. "We're taking them over to the federal judge in Fort Smith."

"What!"

"We'll tell him what happened and show him Osceola's body with the bullet in his back. Then he can decide if we should hang."

"Hang!" Houston's eyes widened. "Good Lord, Blue, Harlan was a murderer, cattle rustler, and who knows what else. He said he intended to come back into the Indian Territory and kill you and all the rest of us. What greater justification could a man have for killing him!"

"Maybe him, none. But the others?"

"They rode for the man," Houston argued. "They knew what they were doing and there wasn't a single choirboy in the lot of 'em! Bury them and forget them, Blue!"

"No!"

Houston wanted to gnash his teeth in frustration. He just didn't understand the Cherokee. Not young Abraham Sixkiller who had voluntarily returned to Lockwood with his pregnant wife to accept his sentence of death, and not this Lighthorse Cherokee who was going to haul five bodies halfway across the Indian Territory to Fort Smith, Arkansas, and place his life in the hands of a federal judge who might even charge him and the other Lighthorse Indians with murder.

"None of this makes sense!"

"It is our way," Blue said as if that explained anything. "You can ride to find your brother and sister now."

"No!"

Houston surprised himself. He hadn't thought out a response, he'd just reacted from the heart. He added, "I . . . my family is known some in the South. And besides, I got a feeling that I can be a little more persuasive in convincing Judge Parker that we acted in self-defense."

Blue just stared at him until Houston blurted, "Well it was self-defense. Maybe not this day, but they'd have come and bushwhacked the whole bunch of you sooner or later. We just decided the time and the outcome, that's all."

"Is that what you're going to tell Judge Parker?"

"Sure!"

"Not good enough," Blue said. "You tell him that, he'll hang us for sure."

Houston blushed. "Well . . . well, what would YOU tell him!"

"The truth. That I lost my head when Osceola was shot in the back and my men followed."

"That's worse than what I suggested!"

"We tell Judge Parker the truth, same as always. We tell him exactly what was said and what happened here. We let him decide."

"Even if he decides to hang you!"

Blue nodded and so did the others.

"You people are crazy!" Houston raged. "You're way too willing to die!"

"You go find your brother and sister," Blue West said. "Cherokee Lighthorse go to Fort Smith, Arkansas now."

"Jesus Christ!" Houston raged as the Indians rode away with five bodies draped across five saddles. He started to rein High Man south toward Tahlequah but then his conscience got the better of him and damned if he didn't go after the Cherokee Lighthorse.

ELEVEN

Fort Smith, Arkansas, had been founded in the autumn of 1817 in order to keep peace between the Osage farther up the Arkansas River and the displaced Cherokee, who were located downriver. It also served as a trading post for mountain men as well as a jumping-off point for the argonauts bound for the gold fields of California.

In the half century of its existence, the town had earned a rich and colorful history along with a reputation for women and even faster horses. At the edge of town was Race Track Prairie, a fast track where thousands of dollars a year were wagered on the finest Thoroughbred horses that could be gathered between Texas and Tennessee. As he rode into town, Houston made it a point to pass the famed racetrack, and what he saw was encouraging. The oval track was smooth, with a wooden railed perimeter, and it looked fast and solid. Frontier racetracks were notorious for being riddled with gopher holes and a surface as rough as a plowed field, causing many a fine racehorse to break a leg.

Blue West informed Houston that, in addition to being a gambler's mecca, Fort Smith also claimed a reputation for dueling. In Fort Smith, duels attracted huge festive crowds and were usually fought on a nearby Arkansas River sandbar that was claimed as part of the Indian Territory. In this way, the duelists could not be charged with a federal crime, since dueling was not unlawful in the Indian Territory. Many a duelist had fallen mortally wounded in the wet sand while, only a few hundred feet away on the banks of Fort Smith, raucous crowds cheered, whooped, and applauded. To survive a duel on that bloodstained sandbar was to become a town celebrity whose status was guaranteed to bring free drinks—at least until the next victor waded back to shore and was engulfed by the admiring but fickle throngs.

Upon entering the town, Houston was impressed with Fort Smith. It wasn't Chattanooga, but it did sport at least a dozen saloons and houses of ill repute, and he was told that the racetrack would test even the Ballou Thoroughbreds.

"But the contest is often rigged and the fastest horse does not always win," Blue West warned. "The horse traders and trainers in this town are known for their skullduggery and they'll stop at nothing to win a racetrack wager."

"I'll remember that," Houston vowed. "Back in Tennessee, we raced the best against the best and it was the sport of Southern gentlemen. Apparently, that is not the case out in this rough country."

"It is not the case anywhere anymore," Blue said. "Southern honor and chivalry are dead. A man who wagers his purse on the turn of a card or the swiftness of his horse also wagers his life."

"So be it then," Houston said, not the least bit frightened. Actually, he had been down to New Orleans and he'd done some gambling on the riverboats that plied the great Mississippi. He'd seen men lose and he'd seen them shot over the green felt of a card and dice tables. That was why he and his brothers had learned to handle a gun so well. And while honorable men might duel, most gambling men understood that in order to survive all that was necessary was to shoot straighter and faster than your opponent. Right or wrong or outdated codes of honor meant nothing. The only things that counted were blood and money.

They rode past the military cemetery overlooking the Poteau River near where it joined the Arkansas. Two grave diggers looked up and when they saw the five bodies lashed to the backs of their horses, they cheered and waved, knowing they'd have plenty of work in the days to come.

"I'll never understand people like that," Houston muttered, casting a hard look at the pair of dirty but smiling workers.

"We'll take Osceola back to the Indian Territory and his family," Blue said, his eyes wintery as they passed St. Anne's Academy, a convent and Catholic church and school established by the Sisters of Mercy. When a group of sisters who had been about to enter the academy turned and saw the bodies, they knelt on one knee, made the sign of the cross, and bowed their heads in prayer.

"We're sorta stopping people in their tracks, aren't we," Houston said dryly. "By the way, who's the federal judge we're going to be doing the explaining to?"

"I don't know," Blue said. "The federal district court here is constantly turning over with new judges. The last time that we brought whites in for sentencing, the judge dismissed our charges and set them free."

"Well," Houston said, tipping his hat to a pretty lady who stared at them as they passed, "at least we know that isn't going to happen this time."

"The judge might hang us instead," Blue said, not turning his face either to the right or the left as he led his Lighthorse and their grisly cargo up toward the fort.

Some members of the crowd were openly hostile. Houston saw anger and even hatred among several of the men that came outside to watch. One shouted, "Murderin' Indian bastards! You're the ones that ought to be draped over them saddles!"

This sentiment was repeated again and again. One callow, pock-faced youth of about sixteen picked up a rock and hurled it at the Lighthorse. The rock struck one of their horses and sent the animal plunging forward into others.

"Murdering Indians!" the youth screamed, reaching for another rock.

Houston started to rein High Man after the youth. He was damned if he'd allow the kid to stone him or his Cherokee friends but Blue's voice stopped him. "No! Punish the kid and we might all be dragged from our saddles and beaten to death by this mob."

Houston ducked the second rock but it struck High Man, and the stallion whirled and snorted with pain. Houston clenched his teeth in cold fury. He took a good long look at the youth and vowed to seek him out and teach him a lesson in manners once they were out of this fix.

When they reached the fort and rode inside, the crowd was shut out. Houston was in for a second shock and that was to belatedly discover that he was surrounded by Yankees.

"Christ, Blue! You never told me that this fort was in Union hands!"

"It wasn't the last time we came here," Blue West replied.

"Well, when the hell was that!"

"Last year."

"Jesus!" Houston said, staring at the hated Union soldiers so malevolently that he was attracting their attention.

"Look straight ahead!" Blue hissed under his breath. "The last thing I need is you causing us trouble."

They were roughly ordered to dismount and to leave their weapons tied to their saddles. Houston wanted to refuse but he knew that would be foolish and he'd be disarmed, one way or the other.

"Fall in together!" a sergeant commanded. "And no talking."

"Who the hell does he think he is!" Houston growled in a voice too low to be overheard.

Blue didn't answer and the other Indians fell into a line with Houston bringing up the rear. They were marched across the compound as if they were prisoners and brought into a courtroom and told to stand at attention.

"I don't believe this," Houston muttered. He had never stood at attention for anyone and he had no thought of doing so now. He slouched and a big corporal in blue came rushing over to him.

"You got ears!" the corporal demanded. "Or maybe you're just stupid. Stand at attention!"

They were the same height but Houston was the broader. In reply, he reached up, grabbed the corporal by both *his* ears and damn near yanked them off.

"Owwww!" the corporal screamed, slapping his hands over his ears when Houston released them. The corporal bent over in pain and it was all that Houston could do not to drive his fist into the side of the fool's exposed jaw and send him rushing into a deep silence.

The metallic and familiar sound of a Colt's hammer being cocked in his own ear brought Houston's mind back to the issue of his own welfare.

"Another move like that, sir, and I'll shoot you where you stand," a soldier grated, his breath hot and stale.

Houston froze. He was more than relieved to see a man in a judge's robe come bustling into the courtroom and take his seat behind the bench. The soldier lowered the hammer of his pistol and stepped back. "Judge Crawford, we got some Cherokee Lighthorse Police here that are full of piss and vinegar. Could be they'll need some time in the guardhouse—or worse."

"I'll decide that, Corporal." The judge sat down and studied each one of them as if they were a strange new specimen of frontier insect.

Houston's cheeks burned. He wanted in the worst way to state his displeasure and even outrage at the way they were being treated but he bit back his anger and forced himself to remain silent. This was Blue West's affair and it was only right that the Cherokee Lighthorse leader—not himself— should state their case.

Blue shifted uncomfortably in his moccasins. "Judge," he began, "I—"

"Your Honor," Crawford snapped. "That's how I'm to be addressed."

Houston's fists clenched at his sides and he had to bite his tongue to hold his silence. What arrogance!

"Your Honor," Blue began once more, "the dead men were cattle rustlers and bootleggers. Me and my men had captured and removed them twice before and we were doing it again when they somehow got a gun and the leader—"

"Wait a minute," the judge snapped, "am I to understand that they were your prisoners and you let them get a gun?"

Blue was dark complected, but Houston could see him flush nonetheless. "I don't know to this day how it happened, but it did. The leader opened fire and shot one of my Lighthorse in the back, killing him. We killed them."

"Your Honor," a smart-looking young officer said as he hurried into the courtroom. "One of the dead men had his throat cut."

"What!"

"Yes, sir!" the lieutenant said. "There's no doubt about that."

Judge Crawford's mouth pinched in as if he'd just sucked on a lemon. "Which one of your men did it!"

"I did," Blue said. "I cut Harlan's throat. He had killed one of my men and—"

"And you slaughtered him!" the judge said through clenched teeth. "Isn't that right? You executed them all instead of bringing them to this court of law, where a proper sentence could have been meted out."

"I doubt that," Houston drawled. "This looks like a kangaroo court from every angle."

Judge Crawford had been about to say something more, but now he turned his gaze on Houston and his eyes smoldered with anger. "You have the temerity to insult this court of law!"

Houston knew he had put himself in a bad fix but he had never been one to back down and so he said recklessly, "Judge, those dead men were murderers. Whiskey peddlers and cattle thieves! They deserved to die. Us bringing them here is the only mistake we're guilty of."

Crawford snapped up a gavel and smashed it down so hard that the wooden handle snapped and the head went bouncing across the courtroom. A bailiff rushed after it. The broken gavel seemed to infuriate Crawford even more than Houston.

"Son of a bitch!" he screamed, hurling the stub of handle at Houston, who ducked.

"Judge, people in Fort Smith can't aim and throw worth spit," Houston said, pushing on and not giving a damn about anything. "And furthermore, the widow of Osceola, the dead Lighthorse, ought to be generously compensated for the loss of her husband."

Houston heard Blue groan and one of the other Lighthorse take a sharp intake of breath.

"Bailiff! I want that man bound and gagged. At once!"

Houston whirled around and the gun on his hip was in his fist. He backed up against the wall and then he turned the gun on Judge Crawford. "Judge, call these bluebellies off or I'll put a bullet through your fevered brain!"

"No!" Blue called.

"Stay out of this!" Houston raged. "Can't you see that the judge here is as crooked as a dog's hind leg? He'll hang the both of us, Blue. We might as well go down fighting."

But Blue West shook his head. "We can't do this."

"We *are* doing it!" Houston shouted. "And there's no time for holding a debate."

For the first time, Blue West swore—at least Houston thought he did—although it was so low that he could not be certain. The other Lighthorse were looking to their leader, waiting for his decision. Houston knew, at that moment, that, had Blue wanted it, the other Lighthorse would have drawn their pistols and killed Judge Crawford—or himself.

Blue seemed to age a little as he stood in the courtroom trying to decide what to do. Finally, when a soldier's hand moved for the pistol at his side, Blue's own hand dropped to his weapon. "Don't do it, soldier."

Judge Crawford was livid. "If you try to leave this court-room, I'll have you cut to ribbons! You won't reach your horses, let alone get out of the fort."

"I'm not guilty of murder," Blue said, "and neither are my men. We tried to do the right thing. We were even willing to face those men again when they returned after they'd sworn to kill us."

"Drop your weapons!"

Blue shook his head. With drawn gun, he went up to the Judge and when the man shrank back, Blue grabbed him roughly by the hair and yanked him screaming to his feet.

He holstered his six-gun and then he drew the same big knife he'd used on Harlan. He pressed it to the judge's throat and the man's eyes bugged like those of a beetle.

"Call them off," Blue said in a voice that was all the more chilling because it was so calm. "Call all the soldiers off and tell them we are free to go back to our Indian Territory."

Crawford was afraid to nod his head in agreement, much less speak. He gurgled what sounded like an assent, and then Blue West pushed him from behind his bench and they were moving toward the door. On the way, Houston grabbed the big sergeant whose ears he'd almost ripped off and shoved him out in the lead as a shield.

"You'll never make it," the lieutenant swore.

"Don't bet on it, Yank," Houston spat.

Out into the compound they went and they were all relieved to see that their horses were still where they'd left them. Only the dead men's mounts had been led away, probably to the stable.

"What are we going to do now?" Houston asked, looking around to see that riflemen had posted up all around them and their fingers were pressed to their triggers, their cheeks to their stocks.

"What can we do but play it out to the end?" Blue said. "Let's get mounted."

Houston knew that they were dead men if they released their prisoners.

"Mount up," he ordered the frightened sergeant in his grasp.

Blue made the judge do the same. Then both of them climbed up behind their prisoners.

"One move and this soldier is dead!" Houston bellowed at the riflemen in their hated blue coats. "Same goes for Judge Crawford!"

All eyes jumped to a gray-bearded United States Army captain who came barreling out of his headquarters, saw what was happening, and skidded to a halt.

"Captain!" Houston yelled. "We brought dead murderers here and one of our own to show he was shot in the back! All we wanted was a fair shake and maybe a thanks for ridding the territory of such bloody trash. We didn't want this."

"Then throw down your weapons and surrender!" the captain yelled.

"Can't do it," Houston called. "Just can't do it."

"We'll let the judge and the sergeant loose at the river," Blue promised. "Or they can die with us here and now. Your choice, Captain!"

If the officer had been young and brazen, like the lieutenant, Houston knew that he would have made a decision fatal to himself and a lot of others. But the captain was a veteran officer. He looked tough and intelligent and he proved the latter when he yelled, "Let 'em go!"

"But, Captain!" the lieutenant cried. "We can't. . . ."

"Soldiers, lower your arms and let them pass from this fort!" the captain yelled.

Houston felt the sergeant in front of him on High Man deflate as if the air had been let out of him like a carnival balloon. Houston deflated with similar relief. It seemed unreal but they were riding toward the fort gates and then passing through.

The crowd that had followed and harassed them all the way to the fort had dispersed, but the moment someone looked back and shouted, the crowd turned and started back.

"Let's get the hell out of here!" Houston cried, heaving the sergeant from his saddle, then taking his place and sending High Man galloping off to the south, through the narrow streets where chickens and dogs wandered among children.

Blue West and his Cherokee Lighthorse were right behind. Houston heard gunshots, and a spattering of wood exploded near his racing horse as he rounded a corner and headed for the Arkansas River.

They were going to make it. Houston knew that they would hit the river, swim it, and then make the other side before the soldiers could get their horses and reach the water.

The only question was, could or would the United States Army cross the river and chase them into the Indian Territory? Houston had no idea, but just to be on the safe side, he decided to keep his stallion running until he found Ruff and Dixie and their new home.

It made more sense than anything he could think of at the moment.

TWELVE

Houston felt a rush of exhilaration when High Man's front hooves struck the north bank of the Arkansas River as he and the Cherokee Lighthorse galloped into the Indian Territory. When they had run about a mile to a high point of land overlooking the River and distant Fort Smith, there was still no pursuit in sight.

Houston dismounted and loosened High Man's cinch. The old stallion was tough, but their flight and that freezing river had taken its toll on the Thoroughbred stallion. High Man was trembling, his head was down, and he was coughing.

Houston removed his coat and began to rub the old stallion, more to stimulate circulation than to actually dry the horse. High Man shook himself and groaned. He was obviously chilled and since he had never had a chance to rest since their escape from Tennessee, he had been weakened.

"That horse doesn't sound good," Blue West said. "He needs a warm stall out of this cold wind, along with plenty of food and rest."

Houston nodded. "It was the river that put the chill in him but he'll be all right once he dries off. I just wish the wind wasn't so damned cold."

Blue nodded but it was obvious to all of them that his troubled thoughts were absorbed by the fix they had placed themselves in with the federal authorities in Fort Smith.

"Listen," Houston said, still rubbing his stallion, "there was no choice once we got into that courtroom. Judge Crawford was going to have us arrested and placed in a cell for the deaths of Harlan and those other cutthroats."

111

Blue West didn't agree, but he didn't actually disagree, either. Houston tried another tack. "The thing of it is, we were owed a debt of thanks for going to all the trouble to bring those bodies into Fort Smith."

Blue looked to his somber Indian companions. He said, "I can't let them bury Osceola without the traditional burial ceremony. I have to go back for him."

"What!" Houston exclaimed, his eyes darting from Blue to the other Lighthorse. When he saw them nod in agreement, Houston was incensed. "Come on! Use your heads! We can't help Osceola or his family by getting ourselves killed over a corpse."

But Blue West wasn't listening and he turned his horse and rode over the hill and into some trees, where they dismounted and removed their saddles. When Houston remounted High Man, the Thoroughbred felt stronger but he was still coughing. Houston overtook the Lighthorse and dismounted.

"Are you really going back?" he demanded.

"As soon as it gets dark," Blue said, stretching out on the dead leaves and pulling his hat over his eyes in order to take a nap.

"Well, I'm not! I went along with all of this so far, but this is the end."

"Good-bye, Houston Ballou," the sergeant said.

Houston swung around to try to talk some sense into the other Indians but they refused to look at him and also prepared themselves to nap.

"You Indian people are crazy!" Houston raged.

The Lighthorse didn't bother to deny the fact. Houston rode back up to the top of the hill and studied Fort Smith across the Arkansas River. What the hell was he going to do now? High Man was not well and going after a corpse so it could be buried properly was idiotic.

But there were horses down by the river. Some grazing, others in a corral near the flatboat that carried many people and wagons between Fort Smith and the Indian Territory. It wouldn't be very difficult to borrow a horse and leave High Man to rest until he returned.

"What are you thinking about!" Houston swore angrily at himself.

But then a thin smile touched the corners of his lips because, dammit, he knew exactly what he was thinking about. He was part of the Cherokee Lighthorse now, at least until they planted poor dead Osceola according to the Indian way—or Houston got himself planted for being such a fool.

That night, on a fresh horse that he'd "borrowed", Houston and the Cherokee Lighthorse swam back across the Arkansas River and rode through the dark streets into Fort Smith. They had spent some time debating where the bodies of Osceola, Harlan, and the others would be kept until burial. They'd finally decided the bodies, since they had been civilians instead of soldiers, would be handled by a civilian undertaker.

"There can't be but one or two in that town," Houston had opinioned. "So all we have to do is ask and break into the funeral parlor and cart poor Osceola back to Tahlequah."

"You make it sound very easy," Blue had said.

But now, as Houston rode his shivering, dripping horse into Fort Smith, he knew it wasn't going to be quite as easy as he'd imagined. To begin with, except Fort Smith's saloons, most businesses were boarded up tight. And secondly, there were throngs of Union soldiers drinking and carousing with the women attracted by the prospect of Union dollars.

Blue looked to his men and motioned for them to ride into the shadows and wait for further orders.

"Let's dismount and find out where the funeral parlors are," Blue said in a low voice to Houston.

Houston tugged his hat down to his brow. Several people looked at him but no one made a connection with the day's earlier excitement, probably because High Man had been so eye catching that only the Thoroughbred stallion would have been remembered.

When they stepped up on the boardwalk, Houston and Blue both sidled up against the Whitney Brothers' Merchantile Store and stuffed their hands in their pockets, just waiting for someone local to saunter along.

They didn't have long to wait. A drunken man that looked to be down on his luck came swaying up the boardwalk. He was humming a tune that Houston didn't recognize and rummaging around in his pants pockets, as if he still had a few coins that might buy him one last drink.

"Evenin'," Houston said as the man grew near.

The drunk had been so self-absorbed in his futile search for pocket change that he was startled. His worn shoes did a little shuffle but when he glanced into Houston's eyes, he smiled, burped, and covered his face with a giggle. "Sorry."

"That's all right," Houston said, trying to appear as harmless as the drunk. "Looks like you're making quite a night of it."

"Do ever' night I get a dollar or two," the man announced rather proudly. "Drinkin' kills the worms that eat at a man's mind and body, don't you agree?"

"Yes they do," Houston said. "I could use a little whiskey myself on this cold, windy evening."

"Well, come along with me if you're buyin'!" The drunk actually grabbed at his arm but Houston pulled it back.

"Maybe later," he said. "Me and my friend are waiting for someone."

"Well, bring him, too!" the drunk said, cocking his head sideways and staring like a puzzled parakeet at Blue, who had yet to say a word.

"I wanted to meet the town mortician," Blue said quietly. "Is he around here someplace?"

The drunk frowned. He opened his mouth, closed it, then opened it again and squeaked, "You want to meet the undertaker . . . tonight?"

"Sure."

"What for!"

"He's an old friend," Blue said.

When the drunk scratched and then shook his head in bewilderment, Blue added, "You see, I need to arrange a buryin'."

"Oh!" The drunk swayed around and raised a hand. "Well,

his office is just down the street four or five doors. He's probably workin' tonight on all them poor stiffs that was brought by the Indians for buryin'."

"Thanks."

Blue and Houston started to leave but the drunk was still talking and following along behind. "The mortician might want a couple of stiff drinks with us tonight. Yessir, them bodies were pretty rank, and that's probably just exactly what he'd like, ain't it, friends."

"Probably," Houston said, realizing that the drunk was a wild card that needed to be eliminated before he caused problems.

"Here," Houston said, drawing his wallet from his coat pocket.

"Why, this Confederate money is worthless!" The drunk stared at it and then burped and gave a thumbs-down. "Worthless."

"Here," Blue said, dragging a few dollars out of his own pocket. "Go buy a bottle for us and save us a table at the nearest saloon. We're new in town so pick the waterin' hole of your choice."

The drunk grinned broadly because Blue had given him a five-dollar bill. "Why, thank you! And yes, sir! I'll just mosy down to the . . . the Bad Horse Saloon and get us a bottle of their finest! You get the mortician and hurry along."

"We'll do that," Houston promised, setting his hands on the man's shoulders, then revolving him around and giving him a gentle shove.

The drunk giggled and swayed on down the boardwalk, humming louder now and after he'd gone a little ways, breaking into full song.

Houston chuckled. "I wish I could join him at the Bad Horse Saloon for a few drinks. I kind of liked the poor fella."

"There isn't such a saloon in Fort Smith," Blue West said matter-of-factly.

Houston did a double take. "Really?"

"That's right. He'll get a bottle but we weren't invited to join his party."

Houston's brows knitted. "It's hard to judge the people in this town since I've spent so little time here," he said, remembering how he and the Lighthorse had been callously treated when they'd first arrived with the corpses that same morning. "But from what I've seen, they aren't much to brag about."

"Let's just hope he wasn't also lying about the funeral parlor," Blue said.

As it turned out, the drunk had told them the truth and the mortician's office was lit up like broad daylight. Houston and Blue could see the mortician's shadow moving against the wall as he worked in a back room.

"How do you want to do this?" Houston asked.

"Go get the others and bring the horses around into the alley behind this building," Blue said.

"Are you going to wait before we get here?"

"Sure."

Houston didn't like leaving but this was Blue's game, not his own, so he nodded and headed back toward their horses and the other Indians who were waiting in the shadows.

They were back behind the undertaker's parlor in less than five minutes. Blue said, "Keep the horses ready to run. I'll take care of this."

"Let me go with you," Houston said.

"No."

Houston bit back a protest and remained on horseback. He watched as Blue pulled his sidearm and then moved over to the back door of the undertaker's office. There was enough moonlight to see Blue grab the door handle and try to turn it. It was easy to see that the door was locked.

For minute, nobody moved, and then Blue West reared back and kicked as hard as he could. He must have been able to kick like a Kentucky mule because the door cracked and two more kicks knocked it in. For an instant, Blue's body was framed by lamplight as he stood in the doorway.

And then suddenly, they heard a shot and saw Blue stagger backward.

"Blue!" Houston shouted, throwing himself from his horse and racing forward even as the Cherokee took another bullet but managed to unleash two shots before he crumpled to the alley.

Houston's gun was in his fist as he threw himself into the busted back door, just in time to see a man go flying out the front door on the main street calling for help. There was a soldier in the hallway, crawling toward the front door and in his wake was a smear of blood.

"Jesus Christ!" Houston swore, holstering his gun and kneeling beside Blue.

The Cherokee clung to him for a moment, mouth trying to summon up words instead of blood bubbles. Houston could hear shouts from the street and then, with a tremendous effort, Blue gasped, "Get us both . . . home!"

Houston looked up at the other Lighthorse. "Get Osceola's body, quick!"

The Lighthorse jumped into the funeral parlor and came staggering out with Osceola's stiff, putrid body in their arms. For an instant, they stared at Blue West, but then Houston was scooping the Cherokee up in his arms and rushing toward his horse.

"Hang on!" Houston called, throwing Blue up into his saddle and then jumping on behind. "Let's get out of here!"

Osceola's body was so stiff it did not hang over the saddle, and it took two of the Indians to keep the corpse on horseback as they scrambled down the dark alleyway and shot out past the cemetery.

"Hang on!" Houston urged, clutching the wounded Cherokee to his breast as he booted their racing horse into the Arkansas River.

Soon they got across the river without drowning but when Houston bailed off his horse, Blue West tumbled lifeless into his arms.

"Oh, dammit!" Houston raged, easing the Cherokee Lighthorse to the damp riverbed earth.

He looked up to see the others struggling to get Osceola's body to shore.

"Dump it in the river, for hell sakes!" Houston screamed.

But the Lighthorse wouldn't do that, and when they finally got to shore, Houston was so furious at losing Blue over a corpse that he was afraid of what he might say and do to them if he gave way to his emotions.

"He's dead! And for what! So that another dead man can be buried on this side of the river instead of that! I don't understand any of this!"

One of the Cherokee climbed wearily off his horse and walked over to Blue West. He bent and picked Blue up, then carried him over to his own horse, where he laid the body across his saddle before taking up his reins and leading his horse away.

Houston clenched his fists until his nails brought specks of blood to his palms. He took a deep breath and then remounted and rode off to reclaim High Man.

The old stallion was coughing so loudly that he was easy to find, and when Houston got the Thoroughbred saddled, he mounted him and rode slowly along after the Cherokee Lighthorse, toward Tahlequah.

THIRTEEN

Ruff lowered his ax and mopped his brow, feeling the muscles of his arms and shoulders cramp. Not far away, five Cherokee Indians kept up their rythmic chopping of logs while two more worked a set of big mules skidding bundles of corral poles down to the clearing, where the Ballou cabin and barn already stood against the lush background of pale spring grass.

This was a fine valley and Ruff knew that had his father still been alive, Justin would have approved of the way this new horse ranch was taking shape. The corrals, paddocks, tack and food barns were all vivid in Ruff's mind. He knew exactly how each would lie in relationship to the other buildings. There was plenty of water and more than enough flat land to build a racetrack this first Oklahoma summer.

Thinking about it, Ruff could scarcely believe how quickly their horse ranch had progressed. They'd found this beautiful site and then, after a great deal of worry, Houston had returned shortly after the new year with the sad tale of the deaths of two Cherokee Lighthorse and his own narrow escape from the so-called federal justice administered out of Fort Smith.

And now, with the days growing long and warm, these Cherokee friends were making this horse ranch a reality. Two of the Thoroughbred mares had already foaled. One of these mares and her colt were to be the payment to the Cherokee for their months of hard construction labor. Ruff did not know how he could have done it with only Dixie and Thia while Houston patrolled the Indian Territory as a

119

member of the Cherokee Lighthorse.

Even as Ruff caught his breath, he saw Thia come swinging across the grassy fields with something to eat in a small wicker basket. God, she was beautiful! As tired and sore as Ruff was from his constant labors, he still felt an inner stirring whenever he saw Thia bathed in sun or moonlight. Someday, when he had this place up and running, they would marry, he was sure of that much. Thia loved the horses and had even taken to exercising High Fire when there was time. It was a real sight to see Thia and Dixie astride a pair of fine Tennessee Thoroughbreds, racing across this big-shouldered valley. Even the Cherokee would stop their work and stare with wide smiles.

Yes, sir, Ruff thought, a man could look at those two beauties and the way this ranch was taking form and feel as if he had accomplished a whole lot in a very short period of time.

The only cloud on Ruff's horizon was the war, which was now in its death throes. Stand Watie and his First Cherokee Mounted Rifles had fought valiantly on conduction operations against Union positions in Missouri, Kansas, and Arkansas. His daring cavalry raids included the capture of a steamer on the Arkansas River. This was soon followed by the Cabin Creek raid, which annihilated an entire Union supply column and elevated his status in the Confederate army to brigadier general.

But from what little Ruff could tell on his infrequent visits to Tahlequah or from what Houston imparted when he stopped by to rest for a few days, the South had almost nothing except Watie's successes to cheer about. And to his dismay, more and more of the Cherokee were shifting their allegiance to the Union. Those who owned slaves and plantations in the Indian Territory were now freeing their slaves in anticipation that they would curry favor when the war was over with the victorious North.

Ruff was still loyal to the South in all his sympathies, and so was Dixie and Houston. Thia, however, had shifted her political thinking and was now convinced that the sooner the Confederacy surrendered, the less would be the terrible destruction of life and property. To Thia's way of thinking, the war was lost and there was no longer any need to hope-lessly waste the blood of any more fine Southerners.

As the war crawled to its inevitable conclusion, Ruff, Dixie, and Thia spent many an evening before their fireplace debating the future of the South and particularly of the Indian Territory.

"It's sad," Ruff often repeated, "that we have General Stand Watie pulling the Cherokee to the Confederacy and Chief John Ross living in Washington, D.C., and rallying his loyal supporters to the Union. The Cherokee are so divided by this war that when it's finally over, we'll be punished by both sides."

"We've got Cherokee killing Cherokee over this damned war!" Thia had exclaimed in anger. "We should have stayed neutral from start to finish. But now that the outcome is no longer in doubt, Stand Watie ought to give up and try to make peace. If he was as great a man as I used to think, he'd be working to save Indian lives, not needlessly waste them."

Dixie had her own independent views, and she sided with the Confederacy although, more and more, she thought in terms of what was best for the Cherokee. "The Five Civilized Tribes are nothing but pawns in this whole tragic affair," she had contended. "They ought to be left alone because they are not a part of this war."

"I'm afraid they are," Ruff would reply. "Stand Watie and John Ross have taken opposite positions and the Cherokee people have lined up on both sides. Being neutral just wasn't possible."

And that was how the arguments on the war ran conversa-tion after conversation, all over the Indian Territory. No one wanted to see the Indians punished for a war that they had tried hard to avoid. What the Indians needed and most desired was peace and time to build their future in this county.

Thia came up and without saying a word, kissed Ruff light-ly on the lips. "You and our friends are working too hard."

"That's what you say every day," Ruff told her.

"It's true. We need some more supplies, Rufus. And we're all out of money."

"We can get by a few more weeks with what we have," Ruff told her.

"We're low on flour and out of coffee. You and Houston finished that the last time he came by."

"Then I'll ask him to bring some the next time he comes by," Ruff said, noting some riders that had moved into their valley from the north. "Looks like we've got some company, Thia."

She followed his gaze while Ruff watched as his Cherokee helpers dropped their work and went to claim their rifles. In this country, it paid to be prepared for trouble.

"We'd best get down to the cabin and get ready to meet whoever they are," Ruff said.

"If it is trouble, we will shoot from the trees, brother," one of the Indians said.

Ruff nodded his thanks as he and Thia hurried down toward their cabin, where Dixie was alone.

When they reached the cabin, Ruff went inside and bolted the heavy pine door, then shuttered the windows. There were gun ports and each of them took one so that they could see danger approaching from every side except that in the direction of the forest, which their Cherokee friends would protect.

"Have you ever seen them before?" Dixie asked, clutching a Navy Colt.

"No," Ruff said, deciding that it would be impossible to hide in the cabin and that he needed to open the door and step out into view but to keep his gun ready.

Ruff unbarred the door and the riders angled in past their new barn and came to a halt about fifty feet from the cabin.

"Afternoon," said a man in a black suit, white starched shirt, and black silk tie as he removed his derby and mopped his brow with his forearm. "Warm day, isn't it."

"It is," Ruff said, studying the man who'd spoke as well as his companions. They looked rough, but not entirely dangerous. "I'd invite you to step down but we're not ready for company."

"That's a shame," the man said, "because my name is Mayor Oscar Toliver and I've come all the way down to invite you and your friends to the biggest horse-racin' ever held in the Kansas Territory."

"Is that a fact?"

"It is," the mayor said. "And word has reached me that you do own some mighty special racehorses."

"I have a few mares with fillies suckling."

Toliver was a large, beet-faced man with mutton-chop whiskers and a gravelly voice. He wore a six-gun around his ample waist and a gold watch and chain. Instead of riding boots, he wore round-toed shoes and his white stockings were stained with the sweat of his horse. He was not a good horseman and sat bent over like an anxious toad about to hop.

Pointing a pudgy forefinger at High Fire, who was penned in a log-pole corral, he said, "I'm not an expert on horseflesh, Mr. Ballou, but I never saw a mare that looked like that one."

"He's a three-year-old stallion."

"In running condition, looks to me," Toliver said. "Is he as fast as he appears?"

"He shows promise," Ruff said.

"I'll just bet he does." Toliver looked at the four men who flanked him, then his head swiveled around and he studied Ruff very intensely. "I've heard there's another stallion looks pretty much like this one."

Ruff held his tongue. Toliver finally said, "And I guess he's probably this youngster's daddy that your brother is riding. That right?"

"You seem to have all the answers," Ruff said.

"Not all of them." Toliver dismounted clumsily and stepped out in front of his horse. "I hear that your brother is making quite a reputation for the Cherokee Lighthorse these days."

"I wouldn't know," Ruff said. "We're too busy building this horse ranch to keep up with anything but our own progress."

"Well, sir," Toliver said, grinning, "I can see that you are accomplishing a great deal here. Do you intend to build a racetrack, by chance?"

"We might," Ruff said.

"Be a poor idea," the mayor of Lynchville said. "You see, between my little town and big ole Fort Smith, we think that's about all the racetracks this country can profitably accomodate. Besides, we got the people, all you've got is grass, sky, and trees out here by yourselves."

"Don't be so sure of that, Mr. Toliver," Dixie said, stepping into the doorframe. "Once our track is built, the Indians will come here, and there is no one that loves to wager and watch horses race more than Indians."

Toliver frowned. "Well, miss, you just might have a point. You see, as mayor of Lynchville, we do appreciate the Indian trade that comes out of this country. We try to be neighborly and offer quality goods at fair prices. And, of course, we like to race against the Indian ponies for the fun . . . and the profit of it."

"Things change," Ruff said, sensing that Toliver's tone was starting to take on a nasty edge. "Mostly what I've heard about your town is that you export cattle and horse rustlers and bad bootleg liquor into the Indian Territory."

Toliver flushed. "You got a bold and runaway mouth on you, young man."

Ruff stiffened and his black eyes flashed. "I say what's on my mind and, in this case, is common knowledge, Mr. Toliver."

"Well," Toliver said, remounting his horse, "what is also common knowledge is that your brother is raisin' holy hell in these parts. He's gonna get the Cherokee Lighthorse wiped out, is what he's gonna do if he ain't careful."

"Is that a threat, Mr. Toliver?"

"A promise." Toliver leaned forward in his saddle. "I heard about those five men whose bodies was brought into Fort Smith. Seems that Federal Judge James A. Crawford has issued an arrest warrant for your brother."

Ruff was not surprised, but neither was he very pleased to hear this. "My brother and the Cherokee Lighthorse are going to stay within the boundaries of the Indian Territory. That means, as you and the judge well know, that they are protected from the federal laws and warrants."

"Oh, bull!" Toliver snapped with scorn. "If the judge wants to send a United States marshal in here to arrest your brother, then he'll do it."

"A United States marshal has no authority in this territory," Ruff said, hoping that Rattlinggourd knew what he was talking about when he'd advised him in this crucial matter.

Toliver just shook his head. "What the Lord—or in our case, the federal government—giveth, it can taketh away."

Ruff held his ground. "I think you've had your say, Mr. Toliver. Now, if you and your men don't mind, we've got work to do yet before sundown."

Toliver blushed and he seemed to have a tic in his right cheek because it had began to twitch. "Well, Mr. Ballou, I guess that you probably aren't going to come to Lynchville despite my neighborly invitation."

"Probably not."

"That's too bad, really. There are going to be some real fast horses and a couple of them will be purebreds, just like that stallion of yours."

Ruff knew that he was being publicly challenged but didn't care. "Maybe some other time."

Toliver scowled. "Why don't you tell your brother that he's welcome to ride that big red stallion of his against some of our top horses."

"I doubt he'd be interested," Dixie said.

"Well," the mayor of Lynchville mused, "that ought to be *his* decision. And if he'd like to come, you can tell him that nobody will be out to nail his hide to the barn door in my town. No, sir, the trouble between him and Judge Crawford is none of Lynchville's business. And those men that he and the Lighthorse delivered were just common riffraff. Probably deserved to be shot and have their throats cut."

"I'll tell him that," Ruff said cryptically. "Maybe he's been feeling some guilt as of late."

Toliver chuckled. "I doubt that very much. From what I hear, your brother just sort of makes up his own rules along the way. But I'll tell you something, he might want to consider mending his ways before someone puts a bullet in his gizzard."

"You being one?" Ruff snapped.

"Oh, hell no! We're interested in horse racing, son. And all the excitement and the money that goes with the sport of kings."

Ruff could feel his hackles rising. "Don't ever call me 'son' again or I'll make you eat the word, Toliver. Now, you and your men ride on."

Toliver paled a little and his men didn't look too pleased, either, but they all took Ruff's advice and rode back up the valley the way they'd come.

Dixie stepped out of the cabin followed by Thia. Dixie said, "We'd better watch for them from now on."

"And watch your Thoroughbred horses," Thia said.

But Ruff appeared not to be listening and so Dixie said, "What are you cogitating so fiercely upon, Ruff?"

"Those races. We sure could use some cash money."

"Ruff!" Dixie cried. "Are you crazy!"

"Just a thought," Ruff said with a quiet smile as he carried his rifle back up to the forest and exchanged it for an ax.

FOURTEEN

Houston signaled with his hand and his Lighthorse reined in their ponies. When Houston dismounted, his stallion shook its head and Houston absently ran his fingers across its neck. High Man had almost died of pneumonia after their escape from Fort Smith the previous winter. If it hadn't been for some Indian medicines, Houston was sure that he would have lost the horse. It took the stallion three months to recover, and he was still not back to his former strength and endurance. During that time, Houston had ridden Cherokee ponies in service of the Lighthorse and there were some very good ones. And good horses would always attract horse thieves, red and white.

Houston glanced at their two prisoners. What he had to do was not going to be pleasant, but Cherokee law had to be exacted and there was no doubt that the prisoners were guilty of serious crimes.

"Those two trees will do," Houston said. "Lash both men up and let's get this over with."

George Bushyhead, the best of the Lighthorse riding for Houston, cocked an eyebrow. "The white man, too?"

Houston understood Bushyhead's hesitation. Cherokee laws were not supposed to be administered against white men. Instead, they were supposed to be taken to Fort Smith or Fort Gibson. Well, Houston thought, justice will be served this time and very swiftly.

"Yes," Houston intened, "the white man, too."

Amos Jenkins overheard the command and shrieked. "Now, wait just a goddamn minute! I ain't no Indian and you've got no right to punish me. Not here and not like this!"

Houston's fingers contracted like talons into his stallion's mane. "I'm claiming the right. I'll be damned if you haven't been warned enough already. Three times you've broken our laws and three times we've escorted you off our lands. You damn well knew what would happen if you came back to the Indian Territory with poison liquor. And when you violated a Cherokee woman, you should have been lynched."

"She wanted it!" Jenkins screamed.

"That's not what Joe Gourd says, is it!"

Joe Gourd looked up, his eyes dilated with fear and bloodshot from too much bad whiskey. Joe was a full-blood Cherokee whose entire adult life had been focused on stealing anything that could be sold to earn him liquor money, then getting insanely drunk and raising hell. Joe was an incorrigible and a disgrace to the people, even though witnesses swore he had made a feeble attempt to keep Jenkins from raping the Cherokee woman.

"What the hell would he know!" Jenkins cried. "He was out of his mind with liquor!"

"The woman's story and his are the same," Houston said, untying the bullwhip from his saddle.

Jenkins began to curse and kick but Bushyhead and the other Lighthorse dragged him off his horse and over to the tree. It took only a few minutes to lash him tight against the bark and gag him with a dirty bandanna.

Joe Gourd looked at the terrible bullwhip and his dark face was instantly covered with sweat. He trembled like a leaf in a high wind and his mouth worked soundlessly. He stared at Houston and creaked, "I didn't do it. I didn't do it to her!"

"No," Houston said, "but you stole her horse and were headed for Lynchville to sell it for whiskey."

"No! I swear I was just going for a ride. I was . . . was trying to get away from Jenkins!"

Houston looked at Bushyhead and the others. He could see they were disgusted and ashamed that a full-blood should lie and steal and then be so little of a man to beg.

Houston dipped his chin. "Joe, you can either go over to the tree and act like an Indian, or we can drag you over there like we did Jenkins. Either way, you know the Cherokee law and the punishment for horse stealing."

Joe Gourd placed a shaky hand on the saddle horn of his horse and then he shrieked and kicked his horse hard in the ribs. The animal grunted and bolted forward but it was tethered to Bushyhead's saddle horn. The struggle was over as quickly as Bushyhead knocked Joe Gourd from his horse with the butt of his rifle. Dazed, the full-blood was lashed to the second tree.

Houston wanted to give the bullwhip to Bushyhead but he knew that would show weakness and that, as their leader, it befell him alone to do this gut-wrenching task.

"Cut off their shirts," he ordered, uncoiling the whip.

His orders were obeyed and both men began to struggle powerfully against their bonds. Their eyes were bugged with fear and their muffled screams made the horses shift nervously.

"According to Cherokee law," Houston said, "a rapist is to receive fifty lashes and his left ear is to be cut off close to the skull for that first-time offense."

Jenkins went wild. He thrashed and began to slam his forehead against the trunk of the tree until blood streamed down his face.

Houston steeled himself. "A second offense of a similar nature has a punishment of the second ear being hacked off along with a hundred lashes. If a man should be so foolish as to commit rape a third time upon a Cherokee woman, the penalty is death."

Houston took a deep breath. "Amos Jenkins, before justice is administered, do you understand the punishment you will receive if you ever rape again in the Indian Territory?"

Jenkins was insane. He kept pounding his forehead against the rough bark of the tree and Houston was afraid he was going to beat his brains out. Much better, he thought, to get this over with and be done quickly.

Houston drew his knife. He walked up behind Jenkins, grabbed his left ear and pulled it out, then sliced it off as neatly as if he were cutting himself a venison steak from a gutted buck.

Jenkins screamed so loud that his gag flew out. Blood poured from his ear and cascaded down his torso. Nearby, Joe Gourd saw all the blood and froze, paralyzed with terror.

Houston stepped back, shook out his bullwhip, and let it fly. Jenkins howled at the sky like a dying coyote.

"Count them!" Houston shouted.

Bushyhead began the count. Again and again Houston hurled the whip against Jenkins's bare back. The first ten lashes caused deep purplish welts and the next ten caused blood to well up and run. The next twenty lashes turned Jenkins's back to raw meat and he sagged against his bonds, quivering. Houston was afraid he would kill Jenkins with the last ten blows, but he knew that the Lighthorse would detect weakness if he stopped, so he ground his teeth and carried out the sentence as the leather whip became heavy, saturated with blood.

When he was finished, Jenkins wasn't a man, he was a butchered pig. He was still conscious, however, when Houston cut his bonds, then eased him off the blood-soaked bark and laid him down on the forest floor.

"The border is just beyond the ridge and Lynchville is on the other side," he said. "We'll leave you water and a little food. Don't ever come back or I'll kill you the next time."

"You . . . you son of a bitches," Jenkins choked. "You dirty Indian son of a bitches!"

Houston stood up thinking that maybe he shouldn't have eased up a little at the end of the punishment, after all. It was obvious that losing an ear and suffering the terrible lashes had done nothing to make this rapist and thief see the errors of his ways.

"All right, Joe," Houston said, "fifty lashes but you keep your ears. Ready?"

"Please!" Joe begged in a muffled cry around his gag.

In answer, Houston planted his feet and sent the dripping bullwhip whistling through the air. When it struck Joe Gourd's back it sprayed blood, and the Cherokee began to dance against the tree. Houston, angry at himself and at the world for having to do this terrible thing to a man whose mind had been destroyed by drink, sent the bloody bullwhip forward again and the Cherokee horse thief danced even faster.

Joe Gourd lost consciousness on the thirty-first blow, and Houston, sick at heart and arm weary, could barely force himself to mete out the next nineteen lashes.

When he was finally done, Houston felt so drained that he had to kneel down and lower his head, gasping for air.

"You all right?" Bushyhead asked.

"Yeah," Houston panted, feeling sick to his stomach. "Cut Joe down and let's get him to an Indian medicine man."

But a moment later, Bushyhead returned to say. "He's dead, Houston. He wasn't strong enough."

Bushyhead extended a helping hand but Houston ignored it. He stood up feeling wobbly and weak. "Let's bury him right here and be gone."

They dug Joe Gourd's shallow grave using spoons and tin cups in their mess kits. Then, they mounted their horses and watched as Jenkins staggered off toward Lynchville, flies swarming over the moving pillar of gore.

Houston shuddered and tasted bile. He had seen his share of death and mayhem, he'd killed men in the Civil War, but this act of Cherokee law had cut into his very soul.

"I need to go see my family," he said as much to himself as to his Lighthorse.

And then, without further words, he reined High Man westward toward Ruff and Dixie, the only family and comfort he had left in this world.

"You look awful," Dixie said, "and so does High Man."

"Yeah," Houston replied, stepping heavily from the saddle, "well, you look pretty good. So do you, Ruff. I guess clean, sober living has something to say for it, after all."

It was supposed to be a joke, only no one was even smiling. Houston's appearance had shocked all of them and High Man was about a hundred pounds shy of his optimum weight and condition.

"We could use your help," Ruff said, taking his brother's hand. "There's plenty yet to do to get this ranch in working order, and we haven't even started to think about our racetrack."

In the fading light of the warm evening, Houston pressed his fine hands against the small of his back and studied the work that had been done since his absence. He saw that the barn was finished and so were the corrals, tack room, and several of the proposed paddocks that Ruff had scratched out of the dirt to show him the last time he'd visited.

"You've done a hell of a lot," Houston said. "It's your ranch. I take no claim nor credit for it."

"No," Dixie said, "it belongs to all of us; Thia, too."

Houston looked from Ruff to Thia and he could see the strong bond that had grown between them. He wanted to insist that since he had had almost nothing to do with this place, that he should not claim any rights to it. But he was too weary and depressed to argue and he needed peace and laughter. That's why he'd come here instead of returning to Tahlequah, where the Lighthorse Police were headquartered and where their wages were forwarded by the Bureau of Indian Affairs.

"We'll have plenty of time to wrangle out our differences later," Houston said. "Right now, I just need food and sleep. Tomorrow, I'll feel better and we'll really get some work done on those paddocks."

Houston winked and Ruff managed a smile but there was something very worrisome in his older brother's eyes. He was afraid that he knew the answer, and that it was because Houston had seen far too much death and violence in the last six or seven months.

"It's peaceful here," Ruff said, wanting very much for his brother to stay and for the haunted look to leave his eyes. "One day flows into the next and every evening at sundown, it makes a man feel good to stretch his tired body and then look out at the simple but honest work he's accomplished. We're building a place that even Father would have admired."

"I believe he would have at that," Houston said. "But you have to remember, Tennessee was where he planted his own roots and to his way of thinking it was God's country. The only land worth dying for."

"Yeah," Ruff said, "I know. But I just heard that General Robert E. Lee got whipped again and the Confederate army is shattered. Most Cherokee are of the mind that the best thing is for the war to just end."

"It might end officially," Houston warned, "but the killing won't stop in the Indian Territory. In fact, it might even get worse."

"Why?" Thia asked.

"Because Southerners will be driven off their own land and some will figure that, since theirs was taken from them by force, they have a right to take some of this territory the same way."

Ruff and Thia exchanged concerned glances. Ruff had explained to this girl why he and his family had been forced to bear arms against a ruthless Confederate officer and his cavalry patrol in order to save their last few Thoroughbreds from certain destruction. The idea that the end of the war might bring a tide of hate-filled ex-soldiers flooding into the Indian Territory ready to kill anyone or anything that stood in their way of taking new land was chilling.

"We'll fight anyone who tries to take this homestead away from us," Ruff pledged before he took High Man and led him off to their new barn to give him grain and a hard brushing.

That evening they sat outside their cabin and Houston poured himself and Ruff tin cups full of whiskey.

"I thought this this stuff was illegal out here," Ruff said, sipping the fiery liquor.

Houston chuckled. "It is, but it's like everything else in life: a little is good, a lot will kill you. We're just drinking a little tonight, brother."

Houston gazed up at the stars. "Besides, this isn't the same kind of poison that the bootleggers sell to the Indians. I've seen that kind of liquor blind Cherokee. Ruff, I've even seen a single bottle of that stuff make an Indian go crazy enough to kill his best friend."

Ruff heard all the sadness in his brother's voice. "Maybe you've seen enough of all that kind of thing. Maybe you ought to just stay here and forget the Lighthorse. I never understood why you joined them in the first place."

Houston was silent for a long time and then he said, "There was this Cherokee named Blue West that I got to know a little. He and I became pretty good friends, and I came to admire him very much. When he was gunned down in Fort Smith the night we went back for Osceola's body, I had to step in and take up a little of the slack made by his passing."

Houston took a sip from his tin cup. "And I think I have."

Ruff looked aside at his brother's haggard, troubled face. Houston was only three years his senior and twenty-two, but he looked far older tonight.

"I told you that I had agreed to give the Cherokee a mare and her Colt in exchange for the help we've received out here, didn't I?"

"Yeah." Houston stared at the cup in his hands. "If we help them train that colt when he's of racing age, he'll probably make them a lot of money in Fort Smith or somewheres else."

"That's what they're counting on. I also told them that we'd breed the mare back to High Fire next year and keep doing it as long as they wanted."

"Sounds fair," Houston said, not sounding very interested.

Dixie and Thia came out and sat down beside them. "There's supposed to be a big race in Lynchville," Dixie said. "The mayor himself came by and just dared us to bring High Fire or High Man over and race 'em."

Houston looked up suddenly. "Mayor Toliver rode clear down here to invite you?"

"That's right," Ruff said, frowning because he hadn't intended to say anything to his brother about the challenge. "But we told him we had too much work to do on this place this year."

"Who'd he say was bringing horses to run?" Houston wanted to know.

"He didn't offer any names, but he said there would be some other Thoroughbreds—damned good ones."

Houston chuckled and a soft smile played across his lips. "It seems a long, long time since I watched a Ballou horse win stakes money. We could use some now, couldn't we?"

"We're a little short," Ruff admitted. "But we'll get along awhile longer."

"And then what?" Houston asked. "How do you figure to make enough money to buy winter feed or supplies?"

There was really only one answer to that. "We'll probably have to sell our new fillies."

Houston snorted with disgust. "This isn't Tennessee and the people in these parts aren't going to give us anything like the high prices we got for our horses at Wildwood Farm. Hell, Ruff, you'd be lucky to get a hundred dollars for one of those fillies! And a hundred dollars won't begin to carry us through the winter."

"Then we'll just have to think of something else," Ruff said stubbornly.

"Mayor Toliver said he didn't hold anything against you, Houston," Dixie blurted. "But he did say that you were riding for a fall."

"Ha!" Houston slapped his knee and his eyes came alive again. "Toliver said that?"

Dixie looked at Ruff with a puzzled expression. "Yes, he did. What's so funny?"

"Why, I told him the same thing! Told him that he had best stay the hell out of the Indian Territory or he might find that Cherokee justice would be swift and not very much to his liking."

Ruff didn't like the direction of this conversation. "Why don't we just forget all about Lynchville and Mayor Toliver."

"Not me," Houston said, lips drawing back to reveal his fine, white teeth. "If the mayor himself invited us to race, I think that's just what we ought to do."

"Houston!" Dixie cried.

"Hell," Houston said, "don't start worrying about that. I'll go by myself and I'll bring back a satchel of money. Just you wait and see."

Ruff ground his teeth and said nothing. He knew how his brother's mind worked. Fight him. Tell him he couldn't or shouldn't do a thing and that was exactly what he would do come hell or high water.

But leave him alone and maybe, just maybe, he might regain his senses. Ruff sure hoped so. Otherwise, they were both going to be riding into an Arkansas hornet's nest.

FIFTEEN

Ruff was awake and staring at the ceiling of their log cabin long before daylight. He kept trying to think of two good reasons why he shouldn't just tell Houston to go on to Lynchville by himself if he insisted on getting himself killed. Ruff already had the first good reason—Houston was his brother. The second reason eluded him but Ruff knew that if he didn't go with Houston, he'd never forgive himself if his brother were shot or hanged.

Ruff could hear Thia's and Dixie's soft breathing as they slept into the first gray light of dawn. But Houston, who was often prone to snoring, was silent, leading Ruff to think that his brother was also awake.

"Houston," Ruff whispered, "you awake?"

It was almost a minute before Houston answered. "Yeah."

"It's crazy, us going to Lynchville."

"You've already told me that about a dozen times. Haven't you got anything new to say?"

"Yes, I do," Ruff said. "What if we're arrested by a federal marshal from Fort Smith?"

"Not going to happen," Houston said. "They're not expecting us in Lynchville. You told them we weren't coming."

"People have been known to change their minds," Ruff said. "Maybe they're hoping we'll change ours."

"Go back to sleep," Houston snorted. "Don't you know that there aren't any good men in Lynchville? They're all just a bunch of drunks, thieves, and outlaws."

"Some of them probably know how to handle a gun," Ruff argued. "And if Judge Crawford has put a bounty on your head . . ."

137

"That corrupt old son of a bitch hasn't got two nickels to his name," Houston hissed contemptuously. "Listen, we need to win some federal money. You know it and so do I. Until we can get this horse ranch established and a track built, we have to do what it takes to take care of business."

"If something goes wrong, we'll be business for Lynchville's mortician."

Houston's chuckle crept out of the dark like a serpent and it bit. "Hell, Ruff, stay here and grow old if you want. You've got a girl who loves you, no reason for you to leave."

"Is that why you're really doing this? Because of Molly O'Day?"

"Hell no!"

"I wonder," Ruff said.

Houston's bed creaked in protest as he sat up and pulled on his boots. "But after we win some stakes money, I am going to find her."

"Where?"

"Washington, D.C."

Ruff swore under his breath. "At least wait until the war is over. You can wait that long, can't you?"

"No," Houston said, "I cannot. Molly was a Southern spy and there were things that she had to do in the North. It's driving me over the edge wondering what she's doing and if she's still even alive."

"I'd go with you if I could," Ruff said quickly.

Houston stood up, a blocky silhouette against the window turning pale gray of dawn. "Your place is with our sister and the horses," Houston said. "Father always said you were the best one of the bunch of us with 'em. Better than Mason or me. Better than anyone except maybe Father himself."

"Nobody was as good as he was," Ruff said, remembering the way his father had handled horses. He'd had a gift that went beyond anything Ruff had ever seen or expected to see.

Houston strapped on his Colt and picked up his hat. "How long will it take for the girls to be ready?"

"An hour."

"Then let them sleep awhile longer. I'll go grain the horses. Are you sure the men you hired are trustworthy?"

"Yeah," Ruff said. "They'll stand and fight if they have to in order to protect our mares while we're gone."

"There are only three," Houston said, "and I didn't see them wearing guns."

"They've got them in their bedrolls," Ruff assured his brother as he reached for his boots. "And I'll help you with the horses."

Houston said something but Ruff didn't catch the words as he hurried and dressed.

When they rode out of their new homestead several hours later, Ruff thought about how this should have been a happy outing. He remembered how fine it had been on race days back in Tennessee. There had always been an edge of excitement and anticipation. Justin would promise them candy and other treats if the Ballou horses won, and they almost always did. The races themselves had been colorful, with banners and streamers flying from the boxes of the wealthy while in the center of the racetrack, the working families had picnicked and played games until the races started. There had always been plenty of food and music. People danced and laughed.

But today all of that was missing. Houston had not helped matters when he'd yanked his Spencer Repeating rifle from its scabbard and checked the rounds before checking his pistol.

"Never hurts to double-check," he'd said with a brittle smile.

Dixie was wearing a six-gun on her hip although it looked ridiculously big. Thia was armed, too, only it was with a derringer and it was concealed. No wonder, Ruff thought, that he felt so tense and dispirited. This wasn't going to be like the old Chattanooga days at all, it was about money, plain and simple. Houston wanted enough money for a trip North, and the rest of them needed money to carry on their work at the new horse ranch they were building.

The day was clear and the air was heady perfume as they rode through vast meadows covered with a blanket of spring flowers, which included many varieties of wild orchids, the vibrant passion flower, and spiderwork, whose delicate blossoms ranged from lavender to pink. Acres of delphiniums were as blue as the sky and showy flowering trees such as dogwood, silver bell, and wax myrtle competed with wild plum and crab apple for a man's attention. And everywhere, swarms of nectar-drunk bees floated lazily, satiated and satisfied while butterflies batted along with the breezes.

It was hard, Ruff thought, for a man to feel low on such a stunning afternoon, but that's how he felt, and his sense of foreboding only deepened as they rode north toward the Kansas border.

"Come on, Ruff!" Houston cried. "Cheer up! After all, we're not riding to the gallows."

"If there's a federal marshal in Lynchville sent by Judge Crawford, you might be," Dixie snapped. "I don't see how you can act so happy."

Houston cocked an eye at her and his black eyes betrayed the easy smile on his handsome face. "I guess it's because, one way or the other, something is changing for me. I'll either win and go north to find Molly, or I'll get into a scrape and get shot. Either way, there'll be no more waiting and wondering."

Dixie looked to Ruff and he could see a pleading in her eyes for him to try to talk some sense into Houston.

Ruff didn't quite know what to say that would make any difference. Feeling dull and useless, he blurted, "We need you, Houston. There are things that you can do that none of the rest of us are any good at."

His smile died. "Like what?"

"You're the man that can get the best racing odds and see that the track and all the rules are four-square so we've got an even shake. You're the one that knows how to make folks think that our horses aren't really all that fast. Without you, they'd probably take one look at High Fire and just refuse to bet against him."

As if he understood, the stallion between Ruff's legs tossed its head and pranced a little.

"Well," Houston said, "I don't think there's anyone who could look at High Fire today and bet against him."

"What does that mean?" Dixie asked.

"It means that I think we're going to have to race old High Man instead."

"No!" Ruff and Dixie both protested together. "He's in no shape to race. You know that. He's run down and he's still got a cough."

"He's thin and not too shiny right now," Houston agreed, "but he's sound, and that cough won't slow him up as long as we don't race him over a mile, mile and a quarter."

"I don't like it," Ruff said.

"I didn't expect you would," Houston said. "But if High Fire is the heavy betting favorite, how are we going to win any money on him?"

Ruff didn't have an answer to that because they sure didn't have a lot of money to put up, even on what he considered a sure bet.

"High Man was eighteen years old this spring," Dixie reminded.

"He runs like a five-year-old," Houston said. "Mark my words, I know what I'm talking about."

"Pa retired him ten years ago," Ruff said.

"Then he's had a lot of time to rest," Houston snapped, his black eyes striking at the land that would be Kansas just a few miles ahead.

There was no more conversation until they passed a pair of birch trees. And then, for some reason, Houston told them about Amos Jenkins and poor Joe Gourd.

Thia was the first to make a comment. "You carried out Cherokee law. You had no choice."

"I know that," Houston said. "At least in Joe's case. As for Jenkins, I could have just whipped him a few times and then asked one of the other Lighthorse to deliver him to either Fort Smith or Fort Gibson. Maybe . . ."

"Maybe nothing," Ruff said. "He'd have been exonerated and a woman's rapist would have gotten off scot free. I'm glad you cut his damned ear off and used your bullwhip on his back."

Houston stared at the trees as they rode past. He didn't look glad at all. His lips were pressed together in a thin, hard line and his expression was bleak. Once again, Ruff was reminded that his brother had ridden the harder, more dangerous trail since their escape from Tennessee. And now, if all went well in Lynchville, he would be riding for Washington, D.C. It made no sense at all to Ruff to do such a thing before the war was over, but then Houston had never done the normal thing, even before the war, when the family was together and prospering.

When they arrived in the early afternoon, Lynchville was buzzing with people. Normally a small town with too many men doing too little except raising hell, this day it was swarming with people from miles around who had come to see the races. When the Ballous arrived, the laughter and joshing died and the children stared at the almost matched pair of Thoroughbred sorrels, father and son. The two tall Thoroughbreds had the exact same height and markings, but it was the youngster, High Fire, that held the crowd's attention.

The serious betters licked their lips and came forward, one saying, "You runnin' this horse today, mister?"

"No," Ruff said, looking at his brother. "Today, we're going to give his daddy a chance to show his stuff."

"A little long in the tooth, isn't he?" another asked.

"He's got some years on him," Houston said as all eyes shifted to him. "In fact, this horse just turned eighteen this spring."

"Aw, come on!" a man groused.

"It's hard to believe, but it's true. Someone take a look at his teeth and tell everyone in hearing range what you see."

One of the bettors, a slim, sharp-faced man dressed like a gambler, stepped forward and claimed that right. He expertly parted the old stallion's lips and then forced his mouth open.

High Man didn't like it and raised his head a little, but not before everyone got a clear gaze at his teeth.

"He's old, all right," the gambler said, stepping back and extracting a silk handkerchief from his coat. "I can't say for sure how old, but more than twelve or thirteen. Could easily be eighteen. He's been a smooth-mouthed hoss for many a year and his teeth are pointed out like a parrot's beak, meaning he must be pushing eighteen."

This time, everyone believed it, as other men who had seen the stallion's mouth nodded in somber agreement.

"This horse ought to be put out to pasture," Mayor Toliver said, parting the crowd and looking up at Houston. "My, my. I didn't ever expect to see you ride in here. Not after what you did to Amos Jenkins and Joe Gourd."

"Go tell Jenkins I'm here," Houston said, yanking his Spencer from its scabbard. "I feel like shooting him if he's of a revengeful mind."

He left Lynchville . . . in a pine box after he tried to kill someone for commenting on his missing left ear.

"Good riddance," Houston said, his eyes moving constantly across the sea of faces, searching for . . . for what? A federal marshal or a bounty hunter by Judge Crawford himself? Houston didn't know. All he was sure of was that if anyone raised a gun, he was going to try to kill before he was killed first.

"What's wrong with your stallion?" Toliver said, turning to Ruff. "He sure looks young and sound."

"He is," Ruff said, "but we'd like to keep the odds in our favor."

Toliver chuckled. "I'd guess once you see the competition you might decide to retire this old warrior permanently."

"Let's see the competition," Houston said, "and then let's see your track."

Toliver jammed a cigar into his mouth and spoke around it, his porcine lips moving obscenely as he continued to speak. "Come right this way, gentlemen."

Houston motioned Ruff to follow the mayor while he held back until the last. If he had an enemy in this big crowd, it was going to be impossible to keep his back from being exposed, but he was going to try.

They rode but a short distance to the track. It was nothing but a oval swath of dirt scraped of grass and flowers. There was no rail and no real start or finish. The track looked to be about a mile in circumference. At least, Ruff thought, there were no rocks or gopher holes that he could see.

"Mr. Zimmerman!" Toliver shouted. "We have some new entrants for your horses to beat!"

Zimmerman turned to stare at Houston and High Man. He was a smallish man, pale and dressed in a white cotton plantation owner's suit, with a straw hat and a gold watch and chain. His mustache was shaped like the horns of a longhorn steer and waxed to pointy tips. He looked like a bleached beetle. Predatory and bloodless. Near him was a bay stallion with a white star and two white forefeet. The stallion was magnificently formed, with long, straight lines and powerful shoulders and haunches. It was deep of chest and its coat had been brushed to a shine.

"Nice horse," Houston said. "What are his blood lines?"

"Lines?"

"Yes," Houston said. "It's a purebred but I can't place its bloodlines. Perhaps Irish?"

Zimmerman managed a thin smile. "French, actually. I brought him to America last year and he's surpassed my expectations."

"I can very well imagine," Houston said, loud enough for everyone to hear. "How old is he?"

"Four."

Houston dismounted. "Who else is running today?"

Toliver quickly pointed out the other horses to be raced. They all appeared to have a certain amount of Thoroughbred blood in their veins. None except Zimmerman's bay, however, really seemed to be of High Man's caliber. There was never any way to know for sure, sometimes the most unlikely animals could run like the wind. Those kinds of "ringers" were the real money makers of the racing world. They were rarely brushed or had the outward appearance of being cared for, but when out of the public's eye, their grateful owners usually treated them like celebrities.

Ruff doubted that any of the other horses he saw fit into this category. Except for one ugly-headed buckskin that was almost as tall as High Man and had a little fire in his eyes. He was getting a lot of attention from the crowd, and that always indicated that he was a horse with a proven winning record.

"Let's set the odds," Toliver shouted, and raised a handful of cash. "I bet one hundred dollars on Alden!"

The crowd jeered and a man yelled. "What odds you giving?"

"Two to one."

"Hell, I wouldn't bet five to one against that bay."

"All right," Toliver said, "seven to one."

"What about the weight?"

"Twenty-five pounds on the saddle against anything that can ride at any weight."

"I'll take some of that money," Houston said, dragging out his wallet. "I'll put a hundred dollars on my horse."

The crowd erupted in a cheer. A man might say anything but when he brought out hard cash and laid it down on his own horse, that spoke volumes. Suddenly, the bettor steamrolled. Each horse received odds against the handicapped French Thoroughbred. High Man's odds stayed at seven to one, but the buckskin, whose name was Jake, settled at five to one. The rest of the horses were long shots, but even so, very little money was laid down for them to win.

"It's going to be a three-man race," Houston said.

"Three-*horse* race," Dixie corrected, "because *I'm* riding High Man today."

"Not a chance," Houston snapped.

"Let her," Ruff said. He had put down his last fifty dollars, and if High Man prevailed, that would earn him $350, enough to get through the year and finish the building along with buying winter feed and supplies. Dixie had bet ten dollars and Thia did the same, which surprised Ruff, for he had thought them penniless.

"She's ready," Ruff said. "And we need as much of an edge as we can get today."

Houston's eyes narrowed. "Do you know what you're saying? Dixie won't stand a chance out there if she gets trapped in the pack. The other riders will beat her blind if they don't actually knock her off and run her over."

"I'll get an early lead and hold it," Dixie promised. "Houston, you said High Man was sound and ready to run."

"Yeah, I know, but—"

"But nothing!" Dixie argued. "I'm sick and tired of being left out of things around here. I mean to earn my keep the same as anyone."

Houston clamped his mouth shut, jaw muscles cording as they rode their horses out of earshot of the crowd to talk and check High Man's cinch. "All right," Houston finally said, "but we can't help you once this race starts."

"I've raced before."

"Not against this kind of competition," Houston argued. "This is a no-holds-barred running track. Damned near anything goes except for stabbing or pulling a gun and shooting your opponent out of his saddle. This isn't the South, Dixie. And despite that fancy white suit and silk tie, Mr. Zimmerman means to win at any cost."

But Dixie didn't seem the least bit fazed. "I weigh about a hundred pounds less than you do, brother. And that's a lot of extra weight for an eighteen-year-old horse to carry at top speed for a mile."

Ruff nodded in complete agreement. If High Fire was their running horse this day, he'd ride himself and weight be damned. But the old stallion needed an edge and he did look to be in the best of condition.

"All right," Houston conceded. "At least this way Ruff and I will both be able to use our guns if we suddenly have to."

"What about me?" Thia asked.

Houston studied her for a moment and his voice softened. "Honey," he said, "you can use those pretty eyes of yours to spot the first sign of trouble."

Thia blushed and smiled, eyebrows raised in a silent question at Ruff, who just shrugged. Houston had never acknowledged Thia's beauty before and, as far as Ruff was concerned, he didn't need to again. Houston was a lady killer and Molly O'Day might never be found.

"Let's get the entrants to the track!" Toliver bellowed, using a cheap paper megaphone. "Horses to the track!"

Ruff and Houston both finished shortening the saddle's stirrups. Ruff threw Dixie up into the saddle. "You're heavier than you look," he said with a wink.

"I'm still growing," she admitted, pushing her budding fifteen-year-old chest out a little proudly. "But I weigh a damn sight less than either of you."

"Good luck," Houston said, looking very worried for the first time all day.

"Yeah," Ruff said, reaching up and squeezing his kid sister's hand.

Thia wished her friend the best also, and then Dixie was riding High Man toward the start of the race. It was all that Ruff could do not to pull her out of the saddle and ride the race himself.

SIXTEEN

The horses were brought out to the track. Houston held High Man's bit and the old stallion immediately got excited knowing that he was about to be raced. High Man's head lifted and he bowed his neck and began to dance and prance. He shook his head and rolled his eyes at the French Thoroughbred, then squealed an equine challenge and tried to bite the favorite.

"Ha! Would you look at the piss and vinegar of that old devil!" a man shouted. "At seven to one, I'll put five dollars on him to win!"

Houston tried to calm the old horse down. "Save your strength you old fool," he whispered.

Alden was just as spirited and much the prettier horse, with his bay coat brushed to a sheen and his tail raised a little. He pawed the track with impatience and struck at one of the other contestants.

The buckskin named Jake had the temperament of an old plow horse. It just plodded out on the track looking bored with the entire affair.

"All right, everyone," the race announcer yelled, "you know the rules."

"I don't," Houston shouted, "and I want to hear them before we get started."

The announcer was clearly displeased but when Houston's eyes bored into him he said, "All right, Ballou, it's once around. No penalties and no fouls. Best two out of three wins the money."

"What!" Houston and Dixie both echoed.

The announcer's brow furrowed. "It's simple and the way

we do it in these parts. The first- and second-place horses have a run-off. There'll be a third match race between 'em if the number-two horse beats the number-one horse. Best two out of three takes the money. Is that clear?"

"No!" Houston stormed. "I never heard of such a stupid rule. One race, one winner. That's how it's always been. No second chances. Once around this long son-of-a-bitchin' track is all my horse will run."

"Then you'll forfeit your bet," Toliver shouted. "That's your choice, Ballou."

"Goddamn you!" Houston shouted. "No one said anything about two out of three when the odds were being set for this race."

"Crowd will bet again and the odds change after the first race," the mayor said with a cold smile. "You in or are you out, Ballou?"

Ruff was incensed and Houston looked ready to go to war. "I bet a hundred dollars and I'll be damned if I'm out!" Houston raged.

"Then get your horse to the starting line," the announcer yelled as the mayor raised his gun.

Houston was so furious that he jerked on the bit and hurt High Man's mouth. The stallion pulled back and almost unseated Dixie. And that's when Mayor Toliver fired the starting gun.

Ruff cursed as one of the racehorses struck Houston a glancing blow with his shoulder and Houston was nearly trampled to death by the horses bolting from the line. A little roan mare burst to the forefront and showed tremendous sprinter's speed as she blasted into the first turn. The French Thoroughbred and the the buckskin were in the pack. High Man got a terrible start and ended up dead last.

Thia was yelling her lungs out and so was Ruff when High Man finally began to catch his stride. Along the backstretch, he whittled the distance down until he was nudging the rear of the pack but, unfortunately, at the same time Alden and Jake were also passing horses and moving to the front. The roan sprinter faded badly, and when they shot into the far turn, High Man was forced wide trying to get around the pack.

"He'll never catch the Frenchie or the buckskin," Ruff said, shaking his head in despair because every dollar they had between them was dependent on High Man finishing at least second.

"But look at him go!" Thia shouted.

It was true. High Man's neck was stretched out like a flying goose, his ears were flat, and he was devouring the track. Down the homestretch came the big Ballou stallion, nostrils flaring. Ruff swore he could hear Dixie's screams as she urged the great Thoroughbred on. She rode flat to his neck but most of the spectators were watching the duel between the French horse and the buckskin. The two were charging down the homestretch neck and neck. Ruff could not imagine how a horse as ugly as the buckskin could keep such a pace but it did, and then the buckskin pulled away from the French horse and suddenly it was a creamy blur streaking for the finish line.

Alden had run himself out dueling the buckskin and he faded badly the last seventy yards. The buckskin flashed across the line and everyone screamed and then turned to see High Man nip the French horse at the finish.

Thia threw herself into Ruff's arms. She was shouting and yelling with happiness. Ruff felt drained and when he disengaged from her, he hurried after Dixie and High Man, the second-place winner.

The crowd was shouting and raising hell. Zimmerman was surrounded by bettors demanding money, and Ruff could not imagine how much the Swiss had lost if he had bet on his own heavily favored European Thoroughbred.

"How is he!" Ruff said, rushing over to High Man.

Dixie jumped down and threw her arms around the stallion's neck. High Man was really puffing. His coat was lathered, and when they walked him out, Ruff could see that the old horse was shaky on his feet. His head was down and he looked defeated even though he had raced magnificently.

Ruff pulled the stallion up and reached for its pulse, which was up under the jaw. "Count me a minute," Ruff said to Dixie.

All of them had been taught to count an exact minute to themselves while another took a horse's pulse. That way, watch or no watch, they could tell exactly how a horse was doing before or after a race.

Ruff could feel the pulse racing. He closed his eyes and said, "Now!"

The pulse raced and Ruff knew it was going to be high as it sped past thirty beats a minute, which was High Man's resting pulse rate. Then sixty, which was about what he'd have expected a few minutes after a race. Ruff counted ninety-six beats before Dixie cried, "One minute."

"It's high," Ruff said, "real high."

Ruff pulled High Man's lower lip down and squeezed both his thumbs against the inside of the lip. He released the pressure a moment later and sighed with relief when the pinkish color returned to the lip almost instantly.

"His circulation is good," Ruff said to Houston and Dixie. "But his pulse rate is going to have to come way down before we run him again."

"That might take a half hour or so," Houston said.

Ruff nodded. A young, strong horse in fine racing condition might return to a resting pulse beat in five minutes or less. But High Man was neither young nor in racing condition. On the other hand, he was tough and hard muscled. Houston had run him down but he wasn't carrying any damaging fat, either.

"You've quite an extraordinary horse there," Toliver said, coming over to them.

"Thanks," Ruff said without warmth. "We sure don't appreciate the way your starter handled that last race. And we are damned unhappy about having to run our horse again."

"Of course you are," Toliver said. "Jake is a marvel of a running horse. I quite frankly thought he'd be overmatched against that French Thoroughbred, but that was not the case."

Toliver looked at the still-puffing High Man. "My advice

for you would be to withdraw from the race."

"Forfeit!" Houston stormed.

"Sure," Toliver said. "Better that than killing that poor old devil. He doesn't look too good at all. Damn shame that a horse that age is still being raced."

Houston almost went for Toliver's jugular but Ruff grabbed him. "How much time do we have before the second race, Mayor?"

"The second race will be"—Toliver pulled out his watch—"in five minutes."

"Five minutes!" Ruff shouted. "You're out of your mind. One hour at the minimum."

"Ten minutes," Toliver said sternly. "That's the custom here in Lynchville."

"Since when!"

Toliver smiled benevolently. "Since right now. Are you really going to try to race that gallant old boy again?"

Houston was enraged and it took Thia and Dixie's help to calm him down until the mayor walked away. Bettors looking at High Man sent the odds against him winning at ten to one.

"We need a diversion," Dixie said. "And fast. Something that will buy us a little time."

"But what?" Ruff asked.

"I don't . . ." Dixie's eyes lit up. "A fight between . . . women!"

"What?"

Dixie looked at Thia, who took a backstep. "Oh no, we don't!"

"Then . . . then go over and slap that powdered-up floozy in the purple dress."

Thia's eyes bugged. "Are you crazy?"

"All right," Dixie said, breaking away from them and calling back, "then I will!"

And before Ruff could overtake his kid sister, Dixie ran up to a heavily rouged lady with a low-cut dress and slapped her across the mouth, yelling, "That's for stealing my father from my mother!"

The woman staggered backward. She was probably in her mid-twenties, busty and brassy looking with hard eyes and a smear of crimson across her lips. "What!"

"You hussy!" Dixie screamed. "Family wrecker!"

The woman hissed like a cornered cat and leaped at Dixie. She outweighed Ruff's sister considerably but Dixie was much quicker, and when she doubled up her fist and popped the floozy in the nose, the woman screeched and raked at her but missed.

Thia came out of nowhere and tackled the hussy. The three women went down in a pile, screaming and clawing. The crowd loved it and charged forward to encircle the three.

One big farmer in bib overalls yelled, "Look at them three female bitches fight!"

Ruff punched the man in the eye and the farmer staggered. He was caught by friends and came windmilling back at Ruff, who neatly sidestepped the man and tripped him. The farmer sailed into the crowd and the men he slammed into began throwing punches.

Suddenly, it was a free-for-all with hundreds of men and more than a few of their women punching, gouging, and scratching. Ruff fought his way to Dixie and Thia. He tore them off the hussy and took a few good punches before he could pull them out of the melee.

Houston was down and three men were beating the day-lights out of him until Ruff, Dixie, and Thia yanked them off and propelled them into the swirling crowd of battlers. The fight raged across the track and spilled into the infield. Picnic baskets were smashed over heads, and so were bottles.

It was a glorious fight! Horses stampeded wildly through the crowd, and when a man pulled his gun it was torn from his grasp and the man's arm was broken.

Ruff spotted the mayor trying to raise his hands as he pleaded for the crowd to stop fighting. But Toliver might as well have tried to calm the wind with his words. And when someone blasted him across the back of the head and knocked him out cold, Ruff and Houston cheered and led High Man safely away from the wild brawl.

"And to think," Dixie said, puffing strenuously, "I started all this!"

Ruff touched her swelling black eye. He looked to Thia, who had a split lip but who was smiling. "*We* started all this," she said.

Houston pulled a towel from his saddlebag and began to rub High Man down. Ruff went to his own saddlebags and grained the old Thoroughbred. Dixie and Thia lugged a bucket of water over and then began to fuss with the old Tennessee racehorse.

"Let's check his pulse again," Dixie said as the fight began to peter out.

It was down to sixty-four, still too high and not falling as rapidly as Ruff had hoped, but it was coming down. "We won't race him until it's under forty," he announced.

Houston winced as a man was cold-cocked by a whiskey bottle. "I hope this goes on for another couple hours," Houston said, "but of course, it won't."

Ruff wet a rag with cold water and began to sponge off the Thoughbred's slender legs and tendons. High Man had always had fine legs, and they still felt good and sound. He watched as the buckskin was mounted and led around in circles. Its rider was a small man in his thirties, tough and grim faced. He was a professional dressed in common workman's clothes that could not hide his true calling.

"That buckskin is a wonder," Ruff told his brother and sister. "Beating him is going to be almost impossible."

"He wasn't even breathing hard when he crossed the line," Houston said.

"And he was picking up speed," Ruff added. "Like he was catching a second wind."

"He's not a horse," Dixie said, "he's a running machine."

"But so," Ruff reminded them, "is High Man."

Houston sighed. "Let's just hope he's got at least one more winning race in him and that he gets off to at least an even start."

It was almost an hour to the minute when things finally settled down enough for people to start thinking about the highly anticipated race between the Tennessee stud and the buckskin wonder.

Mayor Toliver looked glassy eyed; one side of his head was caked with drying blood. The announcer was cradling his belly and rocking back and forth in obvious pain. His paper megaphone was flatter than a newspaper and half-buried in the dirt track.

"We've got a few more minutes," Ruff said. "Dixie, let's take another pulse."

It was down to thirty-six and Ruff expelled a deep breath. "He's okay to race."

Thia beamed and Houston looked hopeful. "I'll get him off to a better than even start this time," she vowed.

"I'll make sure that you do," Houston said, heading for Mayor Toliver.

"He'll strangle him until High Man is in a good starting position," Ruff said with a tight smile.

"Is he going to be able to run like the last time?" people asked as Dixie mounted and the chestnut Thoroughbred was led through the bloodied crowd toward the starting line.

"He'll run," Ruff kept saying to the questioners. "He'll run even better with a fair start."

The crowd of bettors listened, but when the odds pegged on twelve to one for the heavily favored buckskin, Ruff knew they didn't believe.

"At twelve to one," Ruff said, looking up at Dixie who was very pale, "we stand to make a lot of money."

"Yeah," she said, "but don't forget that even if we win this one, we'll still have to race and win a final time before we're two out of three and declared the victor."

"I know," Ruff said, watching the jockey on the buckskin. The man kept glancing over at Dixie, and there was a look of pure meanness in his eyes. And then Ruff noticed that he was holding a riding crop. A *long* riding crop.

"Damn!" Ruff whispered.

"What's the matter?" Thia asked.

"He's got a riding crop and I'll bet he'll use it on you if he starts to fall behind."

Dixie paled a little. "I'll just have to stay out in front."

"Maybe I can help a little," Ruff said. "Here, Thia. You lead High Man up to the start."

"Me?" She looked panicked.

"He's a gentleman," Ruff assured the Cherokee girl. "Just make sure that he's pointed up the track when the gun goes off."

Thia nodded. She'd been riding the Ballou Thoroughbreds, even racing the younger mares against Dixie in fun and proving that she was an excellent horsewoman. Not as good as Dixie, but still very, very good and getting better all the time.

Houston planted himself next to Toliver and Ruff saw his brother lean over to the mayor and whisper something in his ear. Toliver's eyes widened in fear and he nodded his double chins rapidly up and down.

Houston will tell him when to fire the starting gun, Ruff thought as he sidled over to the buckskin and its jockey, trying to act as if he were just wanting to get a clear view of the start of the race.

When the horses were ready, Mayor Toliver raised his gun. The crowd tensed. Ruff jumped forward and used his thumb to goose the buckskin between its powerful hind legs. Up close under the tail where the skin puckered. Jake snorted and whirled around, his forequarters swinging completely off the ground, and that's when Houston could be heard to order, "Fire!"

The starting gun went off and this time High Man was off like a rocket. The jockey screeched and sawed the normally placid buckskin around to the starting line. He brought the riding crop down hard against the buckskin's rump and the animal reared back and then charged forward.

The buckskin named Jake was a scorcher off the starting line but by the time he got to the first turn, High Man was running smooth and easy down the backstretch with the same old beautiful and seemingly effortless stride that had always filled their father with such joy.

The crowd was going wild as the buckskin began to close

the gap. Dixie whipped her head around and saw the buckskin coming on, and she flattened a little lower against High
Man's withers and kept him running.

"Is he going to get overtaken!" Thia cried, grabbing Ruff's
arm as the buckskin flew down the backstretch like an aveng-
ing angel.

Ruff held his tongue a moment. He looked to Houston.
Their eyes locked and then Ruff looked back to the track as
the buckskin steadily moved up on High Man. Dixie glanced
over her shoulder again, and then Ruff smiled because he
saw her loosen up on the reins a little, giving the Tennessee
stallion a little more stride.

High Man surged forward and the buckskin kept nibbling
at the distance that separated him from the stallion, but it
was clear to everyone as High Man tore through the final
turn and came down the homestretch that he was running
easy and would win by a comfortable length or two.

When High Man crossed the finish line, all hell broke
loose. Those who had betted heavily on the buckskin were,
of course, rabid about what Ruff had done to ruin their
horse's start. The few who'd bet on High Man were grinning,
guffawing, and in fine spirits.

"Nice race," Ruff called as he, Thia, and Houston ran to
High Man's side. "How did he do?"

"I held him in all the way," Dixie said. "I wanted to save
everything I could for the last race. We could have beat Jake
by five or six lengths if we'd tried."

"Good move," Houston said, hugging his sister. "It looked
to everyone that High Man was giving it everything he had,
and that will keep him the heavy underdog."

"Let's take his pulse," Ruff said, reaching up and finding the artery that ran along the inside of each jawbone.
"Ready?"

"I'll take the count," Houston said.

They counted and when Houston snapped, "Time!" Ruff
grinned. "Dixie, you must have held him in even more than
you knew. He's only at pumping at sixty-six."

Dixie beamed and Houston even smiled, for they all knew

that that low pulse rate meant that the stallion had not at all extended himself.

"I have disqualified you!" Toliver shouted, pointing a finger at Ruff. "You are out of this contest!"

Houston pulled his six-gun and cocked it at the mayor. "Think again, mister. We were cheated on the first race by you, the second race we just returned the favor. The third race will settle the issue."

Toliver had his friends, and some of them were hard gunmen, but the excited crowd was so vocal in support of a third and deciding race that the mayor, even if a gun hadn't been pointed at his head, had to back down.

This time High Man was given all the time he needed, and when the horses were brought to the track, the air had turned very serious and the odds were unchanged.

"Just a minute," Ruff said as someone tried to block his path to the buckskin. "I just want a word with this man riding Jake."

The jockey glared down at Ruff. He was older than Ruff had thought and his face was scarred, probably from the same kind of riding crop he intended to use on Dixie's pretty, unspoiled face.

"Mister," Ruff said, "you ride a fair race. If you even so much as touch my horse or my sister, I'll cut that whip arm off at the shoulder!" Ruff patted the big bowie knife at his belt. "You understand me?"

The jockey was a tough veteran, but looking into Ruff's black eyes, he lost his nerve and dipped his chin. "Fair race," he whispered.

"Yeah," Ruff said. "Fair race, winner take all. And one more thing, don't you dare beat the stuffing out of that buckskin when you come down the homestretch running second."

"What the hell difference would it mean to you!"

"I like horses," Ruff said. "I'll whip you twice for every once you whip the buckskin."

The jockey wanted to say something. His mouth worked and he tried, but in the end he just bit his lower lip and headed for the starting line.

The start was fair, although with Houston hovering over Mayor Toliver, he made sure that High Man had the better position and was actually moving across the starting line when the gun went off.

High Man had always had an exceptionally good start, but the buckskin's was fabulous. By the time they hit the first turn, the horses were racing neck and neck, but Jake had the outside and Ruff knew that the buckskin was working harder. It had a powerful but choppy stride. Its pale legs moved like pistons while High Man seemed to glide like a duck landing on a pond. Down the backstretch the buckskin's youth served it well and it pulled a half length ahead.

The crowd was going insane and Ruff felt that he could hardly breathe. If the buckskin got to the inside rail ahead of High Man, the race was lost. But almost as he began to be sure this would happen, the stallion seemed to catch a second wind and edged up. The spectators saw and they cheered wildly as the horses thundered into the last turn and came out with High Man in the lead.

It was insane the way that old stallion was running. Ruff's vision blurred with tears of emotion to see the old boy, with his ears flat, his legs and mane flying, come sailing toward the finish line. His throat ached to see little Dixie making the ride of her life, and he could hear both riders shouting encouragement at their mounts.

"Jesus," Ruff whispered in awe of both horses and riders. "Even back home, it was never better."

"Will he win!" Thia cried, jumping up and down.

Ruff scrubbed his eyes dry and croaked, "I don't know."

High Man knew and so did Dixie as the Thoroughbred held the slimmest of leads and shot across the finish line just a nose ahead of the buckskin.

Houston threw his arms around Ruff and Dixie and they began to dance and jump up and down, shouting with joy.

A moment later, they were part of the crowd that surged off after the victorious stallion and the girl.

Ruff threw his arms around High Man and hugged the stallion with all his might. High Man nuzzled him and listened as Ruff talked horse talk, telling the animal with his voice alone how proud he was of his race and how he knew his father would be proud, too, if he were still alive.

When things finally settled down a little, the crowd led the procession back to the starting line, and Ruff heard the buckskin's jockey whisper to him, "If I'd have gone to the whip, we'd have won the race."

"The horse might have won," Ruff retorted, "but you'd have lost."

The jockey flushed with anger. "You won't live to keep that money," he rasped. Before Ruff could grab the little man, he disappeared into the crowd.

"Let's get our winnings and get back to the Indian Territory!" Ruff said anxiously to his brother.

But Houston was celebrating. He had a bottle in his fist and he was grinning from ear to ear. "Don't be crazy! This is the first time since . . . since leaving Tennessee that we've had a real reason to celebrate! So let's do it!"

Ruff grabbed Houston and went head to head with his brother. In a few terse words, he told the man what the jockey had said before disappearing.

"Sour grapes!" Houston cried, lifting his bottle to the sky.

Ruff looked to Dixie and Thia. His anxiety must have shown very clearly because the laughter died in their eyes and without saying a single word to either one, they knew that winning this horse race was only the beginning—staying alive long enough to get back to their homestead with their money was going to be the real life-and-death challenge.

SEVENTEEN

Dixie, Ruff, and Thia were ready to put Lynchville, Kansas, in their dust. High Man had been rubbed down, fed, and watered, so he was sufficiently recovered to travel. It was almost sundown and the western sky was a collage of crimson and gold. The problem was Houston. At this very moment, he was surrounded by a crowd of admirers who hung on his every word as he extolled the many virtues of the Ballou Thoroughbred bloodline.

"My father knew what he was doing when he wagered everything he owned against that first great foundation stallion. His name was High Dancer and I have to admit that he was an English horse—but that can't be held entirely against him," Houston added with a wink that brought chuckles.

Houston took a swig of whiskey. "More often than not, High Dancer begat sons and daughters possessed of his own blazing speed. And if you look at the young stallion my brother is riding, High Fire, you'll see the spitting image of that first English Thoroughbred my father won in a card game back in 1832."

"Damned fine horses," a man said with admiration.

"You bet they are," Houston replied. "And we've got some mares and their offspring at our new ranch down in the Indian Territory that'll make your eyes bug because they're so handsome. High Man is a proven sire and you've all just seen what a wonder horse he still is on the racetrack despite his advanced years."

"What's your breeding fee?" a tall, hatchet-faced man wearing a stovepipe hat asked.

"In Tennessee, High Man got a hundred dollars with a money-back guarantee of a healthy foal on the ground."

The crowd murmured with surprise. No one had ever heard of such a high stud fee—not in Kansas.

"And, gentlemen, I'll tell you something else," Houston said, wagging his forefinger, "my father was damned selective about who he'd breed that stallion to. Only the best."

"There ain't no 'best' out this far in the West," the hatchet-faced man complained. "Most of what we own is grade horses with some mustang blood in 'em. But some like that buckskin gelding can sure run a lick."

"Well," Houston said boastfully, "there is running and there is running, as you clearly saw today. Now, I suppose, if you brought a good but common grade mare to Ballou Farms for servicing, we'd charge, oh, say, fifty dollars."

"Ballou Farms?" Ruff mouthed, having never heard the name before.

"Ballou Farms," Houston repeated solemnly.

A gambler said, "Why, mister, in this country, you can buy three, maybe even four good horses for that much money. You ain't going to get no fifty dollars for a stud fee."

"Oh yes, we will," Houston argued. "You think about how much money me and my family won today. Think about it, sir!"

The gambler looked offended. "You got real good odds today. It won't happen again in Lynchville."

"Maybe so, maybe not," Houston said, dragging out a thick roll of greenback dollars. "But who cares, man! Today I won twelve hundred dollars! Twelve hundred!"

Everyone stared, especially the gambler. It was more money than most had seen in their entire lives. Houston just held it out for them to admire for a moment or two.

"Sometimes," he said, his voice low and almost confidential, "you can breed a pretty average mare to an extraordinary sire like High Man and wind up with a pure speed burner. A flier that will make you rich. Richer than you could ever be in your wildest dreams as a common working man. That's why, if you've got a mare that has any quality at all, you owe it to yourselves to beg, steal, or borrow fifty dollars and breed her to our stallion. To the great High Man!"

Ruff overheard all this and he could not help but admire the way Houston could weave a spell over the crowd. Ruff had seen his brother do this before and there was no doubt whatsoever that Houston was the most persuasive of all the Ballou men. So great was his talent that it was not uncommon for some among his audience to run for their grade mares and come dragging them back wanting High Fire to breed them right on the racetrack.

But not today. Not even when one of the men said, "I got a little mare that can run the legs off most horses. She's short but fast and she's in heat right now, by gawd! Why, coupled with your famous stallion, I'll just bet that she'd throw a hell of a runnin' horse."

"I bet she would, too," Houston said.

"Not today," Ruff interrupted, stepping into the circle. "High Man has run three hard races and he's tuckered out."

"Too tuckered out to mount my mare!" The man, a short fellow with a bushy red beard and a nervous tick, chortled, "Ha! Just wait until that old bugger gets a whiff of my Molly mare's sweet behind! He'll rise to the occasion or my name ain't Lucifer Andrews!"

This set all of them to laughing, and Houston looked expectantly at Ruff. "Fifty dollars and it won't take but fifteen minutes or less, Ruff."

Ruff's reply was flat and uncompromising. "No."

Houston flushed with anger and embarrassment. "Now, wait just a damn minute here, Ruff. That old horse belongs as much to me as he does to you!"

"Fifty dollars and he can breed his mare to High Fire, but not High Man," Ruff said. "The old fella is played out. He could pull muscles or just get kicked and suffer bad injuries."

"But . . ."

Ruff took his brother's arm. "We're all exhausted, Houston. Thia, Dixie, and I are ready to head home. I sure would like it if you came along—just in case anything happened to High Man and we needed your help."

Houston had been about to get angry but Ruff's last words changed all that. "You think he's really in trouble?"

"Probably not, but he is eighteen and he needs to get home."

"Maybe you folks ought to stay over a day or two and rest him up," a man in a cheap suit said. "We got a decent livery and—"

"No," Ruff said, because the last thing he wanted was to remain in Lynchville a minute longer than was necessary. He had not seen Mayor Toliver and his henchmen since after the race, and that was troubling, to say the least. Even now they could be arming themselves and getting ready to provoke a gun battle, which Ruff knew neither he nor Houston would likely survive.

"Why not?" Houston asked. "Sounds like a good idea to me."

"We're leaving," Ruff said, his patience snapping like twine. "Come or stay, it's your choice."

Houston frowned. "If you take High Man, what am I supposed to ride?"

"Buy a horse." Ruff pinned his brother with his eyes. "At least that way you won't gamble or drink all the money up and have nothing to show for it."

Houston flushed and his fists doubled at his sides. When he spoke, his voice cut like a blade. "You'd best be careful of your words, little brother."

"I got no more words for you," Ruff said. "I spoke my peace, you've spoken yours. So long."

Ruff turned on his heel and marched back to the women and the Ballou horses. "Let's ride," he said, swinging onto High Fire."

"Are we just going to abandon Houston to this pack of wolves!" Dixie cried.

"He's been warned," Ruff said, tying a lead rope to High Man and to his saddle horn. "And he knows damned good and well the kind of trouble he's going to get himself into with whiskey and all that money."

"Then . . ."

"Mount up!" Ruff commanded in anger. "Houston is a man full grown and he'll make up his own mind about things."

Dixie and Thia exchanged glances and then they mounted their mares. Ruff didn't look back as he rode south but he was sure that Houston was watching him with angry, bloodshot eyes.

Sooner or later, Ruff thought, Houston is going to have to start using his head more and his gullet a damn sight less.

Despite High Man's obvious weariness and their own concern, they rode without stopping until they arrived back at their homestead. Ruff was dog tired and so were the women, but they took good care of their weary horses.

"I'm going to bury my winnings out behind the horse barn," Ruff said. "Just in case we do have visitors from Lynchville eager to get it back before we can spend it."

Both Dixie and Thia agreed that this sounded like a very good idea so Ruff took their money and buried with his own. All together, it amounted to over eight hundred dollars. As Ruff buried the money, he thought that they would never again be twelve-to-one underdogs in this part of the country. No, Sir! The word would travel far and wide that the people of Lynchville, and especially their greedy mayor, had gotten skinned royally. They'd put a Ballou horse as a terrible underdog and they'd paid the price.

Lynchville would be the laughingstock of this part of the country, and as soon as its citizens realized this, they'd quit admiring the Ballou bloodlines and start hating them with a passion.

"The money is buried behind the barn, right at the center of the foundation."

"Why are you telling us?" Dixie said, starting a fire to prepare some hot food.

"Just in case." Ruff saw no need to elaborate. All morning he'd kept looking to the north, hoping to see his damn fool brother.

Thia must have seen the worry in Ruff's eyes because she came over to hug him. "Maybe we're just imagining things that will never happen."

"Maybe," Ruff said, "but it doesn't hurt to prepare for the worst, even when you hope for the best."

The Cherokee came back soon after and went back to work on the paddock fences, cutting poles and hauling them down to the valley. Ruff, Dixie, and Thia lay down and went to sleep almost as soon as their heads touched their pillows.

It must have been about noon when they heard a shout from the fields and it was followed by a barrage of gunfire.

Ruff sat bolt upright and grabbed for his holstered Colt. He raced to the window in time to see Houston on a badly flagging horse come galloping up to their cabin. He'd been in a fight and his clothes were hanging from him in tatters. One eye was swelled completely shut and his lip was caked with blood. When he barged in the cabin door, he reeked of whiskey and he looked wild and a little crazy.

"What's wrong!" Ruff demanded.

"They're coming," Houston said, jumping back outside and hollering at the Cherokee who were building fences to drop their tools and go into hiding.

"Toliver?" Ruff asked.

"That's right. And a whole bunch more."

"They got your money, didn't they," Ruff said, unable to keep an edge of accusation out of his voice.

"Hell no!" Houston had lost his hat and now he ran his fingers through his long, black hair. He patted his bulging pants pockets. "Not the most of it, at least."

Ruff glanced back to see Thia and Dixie come hurrying outside. He turned back to his brother. "What do you suggest we do?"

"Fight 'em! Otherwise, they'll burn this place to the ground."

"How many?"

"I don't know." Houston swallowed. "Maybe ten. A dozen. No more than that."

Ruff looked up at the Cherokee, who had snatched up their rifles and, instead of hiding, were hurrying down toward the cabin. There were only three but that made the odds tolerable.

"All right," Ruff said. "But we're going to need some help. Dixie, I want you and Thia to ride for Tahlequah and bring the Cherokee Lighthorse."

"We can't leave you and Houston here!"

"You have to," Ruff said. "There's no choice. We'll either kill Toliver and his men or we'll hole up in the cabin and stand them off until the Lighthorse arrive."

"It's either that," Houston said, "or they'll burn this place to the ground same as Sherman's Yanks did to Wildwood after we left."

Dixie swallowed. "All right."

"Can't I stay?" Thia pleaded.

"No," Ruff said. "I want you both out of this. Now, please don't argue. Just saddle a horse and ride."

Thia heard the urgency in Ruff's voice and went racing toward the barn after Dixie. Ruff and Houston met the full-blood Cherokees who'd been working and Houston said, "This fight has nothing to do with you. My advice is to go away."

But the Cherokee shook their heads, dark faces rigid with determination. "All right then," Ruff said. "Let's pick our firing positions and if we have to fall back toward the cabin, let's make sure that no one is left uncovered."

Dixie rode High Fire and because they feared that the men from Lynchville might actually shoot High Man in revenge for winning so much money, they took the old stallion as well. Thia looked very afraid but Ruff managed a smile as she was riding off.

Houston had managed to keep his Spencer rifle and now he headed for the barn yelling, "I'll be damned if they'll get any of the mares or their offspring!"

Ruff stayed with the cabin and checked every weapon they owned, then laid them each out on the table, ready for quick use. The full-blood Cherokee just vanished into the woods and Ruff knew they hoped to catch the men from Lynchville in a murderous cross fire.

It was nearly an hour before they heard the sound of hoofbeats, and then, suddenly, Toliver and his gang came bursting out of the trees, firing at the cabin.

Ruff laid his Springfield rifle across the windowsill and took aim. He was just about to squeeze his trigger when Houston's rifle boomed and Mayor Toliver's lower jaw vanished in a spray of blood and fragments of bone. Ruff swung his rifle sideways, aimed, and drilled the gambler he'd seen Houston speaking to before. The man's death cry brought the charge to a halt, and then the Cherokee up in the trees opened fire.

There were more than a dozen men in the gang from Lynchville, but by the time the first devastating volley ended, only half of them were still in their saddles. Ruff yanked his Army Colt out of his holster and opened fire on a man who was shooting wildly and hollering for the others to take cover.

The rider slapped at his forehead as if he'd been mosquito bitten, and when he pulled his hand away, he stared at a smear of bright red blood. Then he toppled over the front of his horse.

Houston was a crack shot and he brought down two more riders as they tried to escape. The second rider was at least 150 yards away and riding low on his running horse, but Houston drilled him through the back of the head and the man pitched off his horse and rolled over and over down a low hill until he came to rest in a ditch.

Only one rider escaped and he was badly wounded, hanging on to his saddle horn with his reins clenched in his teeth.

One of the Cherokee looked to Houston and said, "Give me a horse and I'll catch and kill him."

"No," Houston said. "It's done."

The Cherokee began to say something, but changed his mind. Ruff knew what the Indian was thinking—a survivor would carry the story back to Lynchville and, sooner or later, more men would come. And they'd keep coming until the Ballous were all dead and their extraordinary Thoroughbred horses were either killed or claimed.

Ruff scrubbed eyes, which burned from gun smoke. He walked slowly back to the cabin and found a bottle of whiskey that Houston had once brought and forgotten to finish. Ruff poured two glasses and sat down at the table.

Houston stepped into the doorframe. "We killed eleven men," he said. "Us and the Cherokee."

Ruff pushed a glass of whiskey at his brother but Houston shook his head. He'd had enough for a while and it showed. Ruff drank his own glass, then started on Houston's.

"Do you know what this will mean for us here?" he said after a long, long silence.

Houston's eyes were bleak and there was a catch in his voice. "I'm going to go back to the Lighthorse," he said. "We'll stay close and if Lynchville sends another—"

"They will!" Ruff snapped. "And Judge Crawford over in Fort Smith won't raise a hand to stop them. In fact, he'll probably send a few gunmen of his own into the Indian Territory after your hide."

Houston sighed. He leaned against the doorframe and rested his chin on his chest. "It's all my fault. I'm the one that's ruined everything here."

"We're family," Ruff said. "We don't hold no grudges against one another."

"I know," Houston whispered. "In these times, we've got to stick together or we have no chance at all."

"That's right." Ruff felt the whiskey already starting to thicken his tongue. But he wouldn't get drunk. Just a little numb. It wasn't every day that a man slaughtered other men.

"What are you going to do?" Houston finally asked.

"I'm going to think about it a day or two," Ruff said. "And talk to Dixie and Thia. They've got a stake in this place just as much as we do."

"Did you like the name?"

"What name?" Ruff asked.

"Ballou Farms."

Ruff managed a weak smile. "Yeah, the name is good."

Houston came over and slumped in a chair. He studied his younger brother and said, "Maybe when I sense things are okay around here, I'll quit the Lighthorse and take that trip north to look for Molly."

Ruff dipped his chin. "This will all blow over," he said, not even believing his words as they were spoken. "All of it."

"Sure," Houston said, trying to sound hopeful. "It's just going to take a little time."

SPECIAL PREVIEW!

Giles Tippette, America's new star of the classic western, tells the epic story of Justa Williams and his family's struggle for survival . . .

Gunpoint

By the acclaimed author of *Sixkiller,*
Hard Rock and *Jailbreak.*

Here is a special excerpt from this riveting new novel—
available now from Jove Books . . .

I was standing in front of my house, yawning, when the messenger from the telegraph office rode up. It was a fine, early summer day and I knew the boy, Joshua, from a thousand other telegrams he'd delivered from Blessing, the nearest town to our ranch some seven miles away.

Only this time he didn't hand me a telegram but a handwritten note on cheap foolscap paper. I opened it. It said, in block letters:

I WILL KILL YOU ON SIGHT JUSTA WILLIAMS

Joshua was about to ride away on his mule. I stopped him. I said, "Who gave you this?" gesturing with the note.

He said, "Jus' a white gentleman's thar in town. Give me a dollar to bring it out to you."

"What did he look like?"

He kind of rolled his eyes. "I never taken no notice, Mistuh Justa. I jest done what the dollar tol' me to do."

"Was he old, was he young? Was he tall? Fat?"

"Suh, I never taken no notice. I's down at the train depot an' he come up an ast me could I git a message to you. I said, 'Shorely.' An' then he give me the dollar 'n I got my mule an' lit out. Did I do wrong?"

"No," I said slowly. I gave his mule a slap on the rump. "You get on back to town and don't say nothing about this. You understand? Not to anybody."

"Yes, suh," he said. And then he was gone, loping away on the good saddle mule he had.

I walked slowly back into my house, looking at the message

and thinking. The house was empty. My bride, Nora, and our eight-month-old son had gone to Houston with the balance of her family for a reunion. I couldn't go because I was Justa Williams and I was the boss of the Half-Moon ranch, a spread of some thirty thousand deeded acres and some two hundred thousand other acres of government grazing land. I was going on for thirty years old and I'd been running the ranch since I was about eighteen, when my father, Howard, had gone down through the death of my mother and a bullet through the lungs. I had two brothers, Ben, who was as wild as a March hare, and Norris, the middle brother, who'd read too many books.

For myself I was tired as hell and needed, badly, to get away from it all, even if it was just to go on a two-week drunk. We were a big organization. What with the ranch and other property and investments our outfit was worth something like two million dollars. And as near as I could figure, I'd been carrying all that load for all those years without much of a break of any kind except for a week's honeymoon with Nora. In short I was tired and I was given out and I was wishing for a relief from all the damn responsibility. If it hadn't been work, it had been a fight or trouble of some kind. Back East, in that year of 1899, the world was starting to get sort of civilized. But along the coastal bend of Texas, in Matagorda County, a man could still get messages from some nameless person threatening to kill him on sight.

I went on into the house and sat down. It was cool in there, a relief from the July heat. It was a long, low, Mexican ranch-style house with red tile on the roof, a fairly big house with thick walls that Nora had mostly designed. The house I'd grown up in, the big house, the house we called ranch headquarters, was about a half a mile away. Both of my brothers still lived there with our dad and a few cooks and maids of all work. But I was tired of work, tired of all of it, tired of listening to folks whining and complaining and expecting me to make it all right. Whatever it was.

And now this message had come. Well, it wasn't any surprise. I'd been threatened before so they weren't getting

a man who'd come late in life to being a cherry. I was so
damned tired that for a while I just sat there with the message
in my hand without much curiosity as to who had sent it.

Lord, the place was quiet. Without Nora's presence and
that of my eight-month-old heir, who was generally screaming his head off, the place seemed like it had gone vacant.

For a long time I just sat there, staring at the brief message.
I had enemies of plenty but, for the life of me, I couldn't think
of any who would send me such a note. Most of them would
have come busting through the front door with a shotgun or
a pair of revolvers. No it had to be the work of a gun hired
by someone who'd thought I'd done him dirt. And he had to
be someone who figured to cause me a good deal of worry
in addition to whatever else he had planned for me. It was
noontime, but I didn't feel much like eating even though
Nora had left Juanita, our cook and maid and maybe the
fattest cook and maid in the county, to look after me. She
came in and asked me in Spanish what I wanted to eat. I told
her nothing and, since she looked so disappointed, I told her
she could peel me an apple and fetch it to me. Then I got up
and went in my office, where my whiskey was, and poured
myself out a good, stiff drink. Most folks would have said
it was too hot for hard liquor, but I was not of that mind.
Besides, I was mighty glum. Nora hadn't been gone quite a
week out of the month's visit she had planned, and already
I was mooning around the house and cussing myself for ever
giving her permission to go in the first place. That week
had given me some idea of how she'd felt when I'd been
called away on ranch business of some kind or another and
been gone for a considerable time. I'd always thought her
complaints had just come from an overwrought female, but
I reckoned it had even been lonelier for her. At least now I
had my work and was out and about the ranch, while she'd
mostly been stuck in the house without a female neighbor
nearer than five miles to visit and gossip with.

Of course I could have gone and stayed in the big house;
returned to my old ways just as if I were still single. But I
was reluctant to do that. For one thing it would have meant

eating Buttercup's cooking, which was a chore any sane man would have avoided. But it was considerably more than that; I'd moved out and I had a home and I figured that was the place for me to be. Nora's presence was still there; I could feel it. I could even imagine I could smell the last lingering wisps from her perfume.

Besides that, I figured one or both of my brothers would have some crack to make about not being able to stand my own company or was I homesick for Mommy to come back. We knew each other like we knew our own guns and nothing was off limits as far as the joshing went.

But I did want to confer with them about the threatening note. That was family as well as ranch business. There was nobody, neither of my brothers, even with Dad's advice, who was capable of running the ranch, which was the cornerstone of our business. If something were to happen to me we would be in a pretty pickle. Many years before I'd started an upgrading program in our cattle by bringing in Shorthorn cattle from the Midwest, Herefords, whiteface purebreds, to breed to our all-bone, horse-killing, half-crazy-half-wild herd of Longhorns. It had worked so successfully that we now had a purebred herd of our own of Herefords, some five hundred of them, as well as a herd of some five thousand crossbreds that could be handled and worked without wearing out three horses before the noon meal. Which had been the case when I'd inherited herds of pure Longhorns when Howard had turned the ranch over to me.

But there was an art in that crossbreeding and I was the only one who really understood it. You just didn't throw a purebred Hereford bull in with a bunch of crossbred cows and let him do the deciding. No, you had to keep herd books and watch your bloodlines and breed for a certain conformation that would give you the most beef per pound of cow. As a result, our breeding program had produced cattle that we easily sold to the Northern markets for nearly twice what my stubborn neighbors were getting for their cattle.

I figured to go over to the big house and show the note to Howard and my brothers Norris and Ben, and see what they thought, but I didn't figure to go until after supper. It had always been our custom, even after my marriage, for all of us to gather in the big room that was about half office and half sitting room and sit around discussing the day's events and having a few after-supper drinks. It was also then when, if anybody had any proposals, they could present them to me for my approval. Norris ran the business end of our affairs, but he couldn't make a deal over a thousand dollars without my say-so. Of course that was generally just a formality since his was the better judgment in such matters. But there had to be just one boss and that was me. As I say, a situation I was finding more and more wearisome.

I thought to go up to the house about seven of the evening. Juanita would have fixed my supper and they would have had theirs, and we'd all be relaxed and I could show them the note and get their opinion. Personally, I thought it was somebody's idea of a prank. If you are going to kill a man it ain't real good policy to warn him in advance.

About seven I set out walking toward the big house. It was just coming dusk and there was a nice breeze blowing in from the gulf. I kept three saddle horses in the little corral behind my house, but I could walk the half mile in just about the same time as it would take me to get up a horse and get him saddled and bridled. Besides, the evening was pleasant and I felt the need to stretch my legs.

I let myself into the house through the back door, passed the door to the dining room, and then turned left into the big office. Dad was sitting in his rocking chair near to the door of the little bedroom he occupied. Norris was working at some papers on his side of the big double desk we shared. Ben was in a straight-backed chair he had tilted back against the wall. The whiskey was on the table next to Ben. When I came in the room he said, "Well, well. If it ain't the deserted bridegroom. Taken to loping your mule yet?"

I made a motion as if to kick the chair out from under him and said, "Shut up, Ben. You'd be the one to know about that."

Howard said, "Any word from Nora yet, son?"

I shook my head. "Naw. I told her to go and enjoy herself and not worry about writing me." I poured myself out a drink and then went and sat in a big easy chair that was against the back wall. Norris looked up from his work and said, "Justa, how much higher are you going to let this cattle market go before you sell off some beef?"

"About a week," I said. "Maybe a little longer."

"Isn't that sort of taking a gamble? The bottom could fall out of this market any day."

"Norris, didn't anybody ever tell you that ranching was a gamble?"

"Yes," he said, "I believe you've mentioned that three or four hundred times. But the point is I could use the cash right now. There's a new issue of U.S. treasury bonds that are paying four percent. Those cattle we should be shipping right now are about to reach the point of diminishing returns."

Ben said, "Whatever in the hell that means."

I said, "I'll think it over." I ragged Norris a good deal and got him angry at every good opportunity, but I generally listened when he was talking about money.

After that Ben and I talked about getting some fresh blood in the horse herd. The hard work was done for the year but some of our mounts were getting on and we'd been crossbreeding within the herd too long. I told Ben I thought he ought to think about getting a few good Morgan studs and breeding them in with some of our younger quarter horse mares. For staying power there was nothing like a Morgan. And if you crossed that with the quick speed of a quarter horse you had something that would stay with you all day under just about any kind of conditions.

After that we talked about this and that, until I finally dragged the note out of my pocket. I said, not wanting to make it seem too important, "Got a little love letter this noon. Wondered what ya'll thought about it." I got out of my chair and walked over and handed it to Ben. He read it and then brought all four legs of his chair to the floor with a thump and read it again. He looked over at me. "What the hell! You figure this to be the genuine article?"

I shrugged and went back to my chair. "I don't know," I said. "I wanted to get ya'll's opinion."

Ben got up and handed the note to Norris. He read it and then raised his eyebrows. "How'd you get this?"

"That messanger boy from the telegraph office, Joshua, brought it out to me. Said some man had given him a dollar to bring it out."

"Did you ask him what the man looked like?"

I said drily, "Yes, Norris, I asked him what the man looked like but he said he didn't know. Said all he saw was the dollar."

Norris said, "Well, if it's somebody's idea of a joke it's a damn poor one." He reached back and handed the letter to Howard.

Dad was a little time in reading the note since Norris had to go and fetch his spectacles out of his bedroom. When he'd got them adjusted he read it over several times and then looked at me. "Son, I don't believe this is something you can laugh off. You and this ranch have made considerable enemies through the years. The kind of enemies who don't care if they were right or wrong and the kind of enemies who carry a grudge forever."

"Then why warn me?"

Norris said, "To get more satisfaction out of it. To scare you."

I looked at Dad. He shook his head. "If they know Justa well enough to want to kill him they'll also know he don't scare. No, there's another reason. They must know Justa ain't all that easy to kill. About like trying to corner a cat in a railroad roundhouse. But if you put a man on his guard and keep him on his guard, it's got to eventually take off some of the edge. Wear him down to where he ain't really himself. The same way you buck down a bronc. Let him do all the work against himself."

I said, "So you take it serious, Howard?"

"Yes, sir," he said. "I damn well do. This ain't no prank."

"What shall I do?"

Norris said, "Maybe we ought to run over in our minds

the people you've had trouble with in the past who've lived to bear a grudge."

I said, "That's a lot of folks."

Ben said, "Well, there was that little war we had with that Preston family over control of the island."

Howard said, "Yes, but that was one ranch against another."

Norris said, "Yes, but they well knew that Justa was running matters. As does everyone who knows this ranch. So any grudge directed at the ranch is going to be directed right at Justa."

I said, with just a hint of bitterness, "Was that supposed to go with the job, Howard? You didn't explain that part to me."

Ben said, "What about the man in the buggy? He sounds like a likely suspect for such a turn."

Norris said, "But he was crippled."

Ben gave him a sour look. "He's from the border, Norris. You reckon he couldn't hire some gun help?"

Howard said, "Was that the hombre that tried to drive that herd of cattle with tick fever through our range? Those Mexican cattle that hadn't been quarantined?"

Norris said, "Yes, Dad. And Justa made that little man, whatever his name was, drive up here and pay damages."

Ben said, "And he swore right then and there that *he'd* make Justa pay damages."

I said, "For my money it's got something to do with that maniac up in Bandera County that kept me locked up in a root cellar for nearly a week and then tried to have me hung for a crime I didn't even know about."

"But you killed him. And damn near every gun hand he had."

I said, "Yeah, but there's always that daughter of his. And there was a son."

Ben gave me a slight smile. "I thought ya'll was close. I mean *real* close. You and the daughter."

I said, "What we done didn't have anything to do with anything. And I think she was about as crazy as her father.

And Ben, if you ever mention that woman around Nora, I'm
liable to send you one of those notes."

Norris said, "But that's been almost three years ago."

I shook my head. "Time ain't nothing to a woman. They
got the patience of an Indian. She'd wait this long just
figuring it'd take that much time to forget her."

Norris said skeptically, "That note doesn't look made by
a woman's hand."

I said, "It's block lettering, Norris. That doesn't tell you a
damn thing. Besides, maybe she hired a gun hand who could
write."

Ben said, "I never heard of one."

Howard said, waving the note, "Son, what are you going
to do about this?"

I shrugged. "Well, Dad, I don't see where there's anything for me to do right now. I can't shoot a message and
until somebody either gets in front of me or behind me or
somewheres, I don't see what I can do except keep a sharp
lookout."

The next day I was about two miles from ranch headquarters,
riding my three-year-old bay gelding down the little wagon
track that led to Blessing, when I heard the whine of a bullet
passing just over my head, closely followed by the crack of a
distant rifle. I never hesitated; I just fell off my horse to the
side away from the sound of the rifle. I landed on all fours
in the roadbed, and then crawled as quick as I could toward
the sound and into the high grass. My horse had run off a
little ways, surprised at my unusual dismount. He turned his
head to look at me, wondering, I expected, what the hell was
going on.

But I was too busy burrowing into that high grass as slow
as I could so as not to cause it to ripple or sway or give away
my position in any other way to worry about my horse. I took
off my hat on account of its high crown, and then I eased
my revolver out of its holster, cocking it as I did. I was
carrying a .42/.40 Navy Colt, which is a .40-caliber cartridge
chamber on a .42-caliber frame. The .42-caliber frame gave

it a good weight in the hand with less barrel deviation, and
the .40-caliber bullets it fired would stop anything you hit
in the right place. But it still wasn't any match for a rifle
at long range, even with the six-inch barrel. My enemy,
whoever he was, could just sit there patiently and fire at
the slightest movement, and he had to eventually get me
because I couldn't lay out there all day. It was only ten of
the morning, but already the sun was way up and plenty hot.
I could feel a little trickle of sweat running down my nose,
but I dasn't move to wipe it away for fear even that slight
movement could be seen. And I couldn't chance raising my
head enough to see for that too would expose my position.
All I could do was lay there, staring down at the earth, and
wait, knowing that, at any second, my bushwhacker could
be making his way silently in my direction. He'd have to
know, given the terrain, the general location of where I was
hiding.

Of course he might have thought he'd hit me, especially
from the way I'd just fallen off my horse. I took a cautious
look to my left. My horse was still about ten yards away,
cropping at the grass along the side of the road. Fortunately,
the tied reins had fallen behind the saddle horn and were
held there. If I wanted to make a run for it I wouldn't have
to spend the time gathering up the reins. The bad part of that
was that our horses were taught to ground-rein. When you
got off, if you dropped the reins they'd stand there just as if
they were tied to a stump. But this way my horse was free to
wander off as the spirit might move him. Leaving me afoot
whilst being stalked by a man with a rifle.

I tried to remember how close the bullet had sounded over
my head and whether or not the assassin might have thought
he'd hit me. He had to have been firing up because there was
no other concealment except the high grass. Then I got to
thinking I hadn't seen a horse. Well, there were enough little
depressions in the prairie that he could have hid a horse some
ways back and then come forward on foot and concealed
himself in the high grass when he saw me coming.

But how could he have known I was coming? Well, that

one wasn't too hard to figure out. I usually went to town at least two or three times a week. If the man had been watching me at all he'd of known that. So then all he'd of had to do was come out every morning and just wait. Sooner or later he was bound to see me coming along, either going or returning.

But I kept thinking about that shot. I'd had my horse in a walk, just slouching along. And God knows, I made a big enough target. In that high grass he could easily have concealed himself close enough for an easy shot, especially if he was a gun hand. The more I thought about it the more I began to think the shooter had been aiming to miss me, to scare me, to wear me down as Howard had said. If the note had come from somebody with an old grudge, they'd *want* me to know who was about to kill me or have me killed. And a bushwhacking rifle shot wasn't all that personal. Maybe the idea was to just keep worrying me until I got to twitching and where I was about a quarter of a second slow. That would be about all the edge a good gun hand would need.

I'd been laying there for what I judged to be a good half hour. Unfortunately I'd crawled in near an ant mound and there was a constant stream of the little insects passing by my hands. Sooner or later one of them was going to sting me. By now I was soaked in sweat and starting to get little cramps from laying so still. I knew I couldn't stay there much longer. At any second my horse might take it into his head to go loping back to the barn. As it was he was steadily eating his way further and further from my position.

I made up my mind I was going to have to do something. I cautiously and slowly raised my head until I could just see over the grass. There wasn't anything to see except grass. There was no man, no movement, not even a head of cattle that the gunman might have secreted himself behind.

I took a deep breath and moved, jamming my hat on my head as I did and ramming my gun into its holster. I ran, keeping as low as I could, to my horse. He gave me a startled look, but he didn't spook. Ben trains our horses to expect nearly anything. If they are of a nervous nature we don't keep them.

I reached his left side, stuck my left boot in the stirrup, and swung my right leg just over the saddle. Then, hanging on to his side, I grabbed his right rein with my right hand and pulled his head around until he was pointing up the road. I was holding on to the saddle with my left hand. I kicked him in the ribs as best I could, and got him into a trot and then into a lope going up the road toward town. I tell you, it was hell hanging on to his side. I'd been going a-horseback since I could walk, but I wasn't no trick rider and the position I was in made my horse run sort of sideways so that his gait was rough and awkward.

But I hung on him like that for what I judged to be a quarter of a mile and out of rifle shot. Only then did I pull myself up into the saddle and settle myself into a normal position to ride a horse. Almost immediately I pulled up and turned in the saddle to look back. Not a thing was stirring, just innocent grass waving slightly in the light breeze that had sprung up.

I shook my head, puzzled. Somebody was up to something, but I was damned if I could tell what. If they were trying to make me uneasy they were doing a good job of it. And the fact that I was married and had a wife and child to care for, and a hell of a lot more reason to live than when I was a single man, was a mighty big influence in my worry. It could be that the person behind the threats was aware of that and was taking advantage of it. If such was the case, it made me think more and more that it was the work of the daughter of the maniac in Bandera that had tried in several ways to end my life. It was the way a woman would think because she would know about such things. I couldn't visualize the man in the buggy understanding that a man with loved ones will cling harder to life for their sake than a man with nothing else to lose except his own hide.